ROANOKE
RAIDERS

Westminster Press Books by
GORDON D. SHIRREFFS
Son of the Thunder People
Swiftwagon
Roanoke Raiders

ROANOKE RAIDERS

by

Gordon D. Shirreffs

Philadelphia

THE WESTMINSTER PRESS

C 280451

LIBRARY OF CONGRESS CATALOG CARD NO. 59-10179

j S55852o

PRINTED IN THE UNITED STATES OF AMERICA

To my niece and nephew,
Laura and Bruce Keene

Chapter 1

I T WAS a bright December day in North Carolina when David Scott and his father rode up the slope of the rutted road in their heavily laden wagon. The steady, rhythmical cadence of metal striking against metal rang through the woods. Micah Scott halted the mule team at the top of the rise and looked down toward the Roanoke River. "Edwards Ferry, Dave," he said quietly.

Dave looked with interest, and with a little fear, at the great metal-sheathed ship hull that seemed to squat in sinister fashion on the ways that had been set up in a cornfield on the riverbank. He had heard many rumors about the fabulously powerful ram *Albemarle* which Commander James W. Cooke, Confederate States Navy, was constructing on the banks of the Roanoke, but he had never realized just how big it really was.

Micah Scott tugged at his reddish beard. "The stories are true then," he said.

"She's a monster," Dave agreed.

The area about the ram was littered with huge balks of timber, iron plating, kegs of spikes and bolts, and all the other materials and equipment required to build a large vessel. The ground was thick with shavings and sawdust. Men worked about the piles of materials and swarmed over the huge bulk of the ram. Sledges thudded against metal and wood while a portable sawmill began to whine steadily, filling the air with the pungent odor of freshly cut pine.

Two large guns squatted near the hull. It puzzled Dave as to why there were only two guns, for he could see three gun ports cut into the superstructure of the ram: one at the front and two on the portside. He figured there must be a port at the stern and two more on the starboard side, and this meant that the ram would require six guns.

Micah Scott held the reins in his strong right hand, for his empty left coat sleeve was thrust into his pocket. He slapped the reins against the dusty flanks of the two mules and drove down the slope toward the ram. The wagon was laden with scrap iron that Dave and his father had salvaged from the wreck of Micah Scott's own little side-wheeler, the *Alice*.

They had been on the road most of the day, driving from their home near Albemarle Sound, to deliver the scrap iron. Commander Cooke was known as the " Ironmonger Captain," because nothing had stopped him from raiding every possible source in the region for scrap metal with which to finish his beloved ram. It had puzzled Dave as to why his father, a pro-Union man, had volunteered to salvage metal from the *Alice* for the *Albemarle,* but he had realized there must be some reason for his doing so. Micah Scott was a man who used foresight and method in everything he did.

Dave's father, a Marylander by birth, had met Alice Denby, a North Carolinian from the Albemarle Sound

8

country, while he had been in the Navy, engaged in making surveys of the North Carolina coast from Albemarle Sound and Pamlico Sound clear down to Little River Inlet close to the South Carolina line. He had married Alice Denby and shortly thereafter had left the Navy. Dave had been born in Baltimore, and when he was still a small boy, they had moved to the banks of the Chowan River, which flowed into Albemarle Sound, to live in the pretty little house that had been willed to Mrs. Scott by her father.

Micah Scott had come of Yankee stock from Massachusetts, and there was salt water in his blood. A skilled pilot and seaman, he had built the little side-wheeler *Alice* to ply the waters of the North Carolina coast a few years before the Civil War had torn the nation apart. There were few men who knew those waters as well as Micah Scott knew them, and much of his knowledge had rubbed off onto Dave while on his frequent trips with his father.

The war had cost Micah Scott the loss of his wife, his left arm, and his side-wheeler. Shortly after hostilities had started, the *Alice* had been returning to Plymouth, on the Roanoke, with Micah Scott in command and his wife and son aboard. They had been to Nassau, in the Bahamas, a long run for such a small vessel, but a mighty profitable one. An excitable commander of a Confederate coastal battery had opened fire on the *Alice*, and she had gone down. Micah Scott had lost his vessel and his arm, and Alice Scott had never fully recovered from her exposure to the cold water. She had lingered on for two and a half years, and during that time she had exacted a promise from her husband that he would not bear arms against the

9

Confederacy while she was still alive.

It had taken Micah Scott some time to decide what to do after the death of his wife, and he had finally made his decision. He meant to travel north and offer his services to the Union Navy, knowing that, with his skill and experience, the lack of an arm would make little difference. But before he and David left the Albemarle Sound country he had decided he wanted to see the great ram with which the Confederacy hoped to smash the strangling Union blockade that hovered off the coast from Hampton Roads, Virginia, down to Cape Fear, North Carolina.

Micah looked at the ram and then at his son. "You realize, of course, Dave, that if that ram is completed and sent down to Albemarle Sound, there won't be a Union vessel able to stop her from wiping out a great part of the Union North Atlantic Blockading Squadron."

"Yes, but the Union Navy has monitors and ironclads to fight her, hasn't it?"

"It does, but in my opinion, not one of them can cross the bar into the sound because of its excessive draft." Micah Scott shook his head. "Davie, this vessel is far more formidable than the *Merrimac*."

Dave's father halted the team near a great pile of rusted scrap metal. "I'll report in," he said. His calm gray eyes studied David. "You look over that ram. Commit to memory everything you can learn about her. You understand? Boys are curious and won't be looked on as suspiciously as these workmen might view a man who asks too many questions."

Dave nodded. He dropped from the wagon and sauntered over to the huge fighting craft. A lean man crawled from under the hull and brushed dirt and shavings from his clothing. "Howdy, son," he said with a smile. "Come to get a job?"

"No, sir."

The man eyed Dave's solid frame and broad shoulders. "You look hefty enough. I can use a boy to carry rivets and suchlike. How old are you?"

"Fourteen, going on fifteen, but I have to work with my father. We just brought in a load of scrap metal for the ram."

"Now *did* you? We can use all we can get. I suppose you're interested in the ram."

"Yes, sir!"

"Some baby, ain't she? A real pet. We'll clear them Yankees from our coast with her all right."

Dave looked up at the overhang of the broad hull. She had seemed big enough from a distance, but close up she looked like a gigantic dinosaur of prehistoric times.

"Yes, sir! One hundred and fifty-eight feet long. Forty-five-foot beam. Draws only eight feet of water, though; enough to make her capable of maneuvering in rivers and sounds."

"Is she all metal?"

"Nope. She's framed with solid yellow-pine timbers and sheathed with four-inch yellow pine. That octagonal shield atop the hull is sixty feet long and plated with two layers of iron each two inches thick!"

Dave whistled. "It'll take a lot of power to move a monster like that!"

"Won't be too hard. She's got two engines of two hundred horsepower each," the man said proudly.

"But why do you have only two guns? She has six gun ports."

The man grinned. "Come on aboard! I'll show you why she needs only two guns."

They clambered up a ladder and stood on the wide fore-deck. The man jerked a thumb toward the bow. "Anyways, the guns don't mean suchamuch. They're good Brooke rifles which hurl a one-hundred-pound ball, which ought to cut through them Yankee seagoing teapots, but the ram is the weapon that'll really put the fear of God into 'em."

There was a heavy-looking wooden snout projecting just below the bow overhang. "That's the ram, then?" asked Dave.

"Yep! We plan to plate it with two-inch iron. That ram will go through wood and iron like a hot knife through butter."

Dave followed the talkative foreman through the forward gun port, noting the thick, iron gun-port stopper that was fastened to the gun shield in such a way that it rested on the deck when lowered.

The interior of the gun shield was a bedlam of noise and confusion. Sawdust and dust drifted about and swirled through the open gun ports. Tools, nails, bolts, plating, and balks of yellow pine littered the deck.

Dave's guide walked through the clutter, dodging busy workmen. "You see," he said over his shoulder, "them two Brooke rifles will be placed one each at bow and stern of this superstructure. But they can be drawn back and turned quickly to fire from either a port or starboard gun port. You see them curved metal tracks set into the deck? The gun carriage wheels roll on them. Clever, eh?"

Dave nodded soberly. He stopped beside the big funnel that came up from the engine room below, passing through the gun shield to protrude above the armored top deck. He had heard plenty of stories about the *Merrimac*, but she had been a clumsy makeshift beside this well-designed fighting craft.

He heard his father calling to him from outside. " I have to go now," he said to his guide. " Maybe we can bring more scrap metal."

" Yep! Like I said: We can use all we can get. Maybe you'd like to sign up as cabin boy. I'll talk to the commander for you if you like."

" No, thanks," said Dave. " I have to help my father with the fishing and farming. He has only one arm."

The man clucked his tongue in sympathy. " Sho? Lost it in the war, eh? "

Dave looked away. " Yes. Good-by."

" Good-by, son. Maybe you'll see us in the sound soon enough, sinking Yankee gunboats by the dozens."

" Yes . . . *maybe.*"

Dave left the superstructure and clambered down the ladder. He looked up at the huge ram bow and the heavy metal plating of the gun shield as he reached the bottom. It looked as if it could do just what his guide had said: go through wood and iron like a hot knife through butter.

Micah Scott placed a hand on Dave's shoulder. " The wagon has been unloaded. I want to get away from here as quickly as I can." There was a worried look on his face.

" What's wrong? "

" Don't look just now, but when you can, look toward that shanty near the sawmill."

As they neared the empty wagon, Dave looked back. A tall, gangling man was leaning against the side of the shanty. There was no mistaking the lank black hair and the straggling unkempt beard, the hooked nose and the piercing black eyes. " Cap'n Rance," said Dave. " What's he doing here? "

" Blest if I know."

" He's coming toward us."

" I knew he would."

Micah Scott got up into the driver's seat. Dave felt a cold chill run down his back as he heard the thud of Captain Rance's heavy jack boots on the ground.

" Scott! " called out Rance.

Dave's father took the reins and looked toward Rance. " Yes? "

Captain Rance stopped a few feet from Dave and surveyed Dave and his father with suspicious eyes. He wore a battered slouch hat with a bedraggled ostrich feather stuck in the band. His short Confederate shell jacket was stained with grease and dirt, but the Navy Colt that was thrust through his wide leather belt was clean and shiny.

" What yuh doin' here, Scott? " asked Rance.

" Delivered some scrap iron for the ram. Salvage from the *Alice*."

Rance grinned, revealing his stained yellow teeth. He shifted his wad of tobacco and spat almost on Dave's boots. " Bootlickin' us Confedrits at last, eh? " he sneered.

Micah Scott looked coolly at the man. " No, and I never will."

" Ain't it about time yuh did? Livin' here in No'th Carolina and making a living off'n us loyal Confedrits. Too bad yuh got only one wing. I'd admire to see yuh conscripted, Scott."

Micah Scott looked up and down the slouching man. " What *army* are *you* in, Rance? "

"*Cap'n* Rance!"

"*Captain* then. You didn't answer me."

"I'm still commanding Captain Sam Rance's Provisional Partisan Company, Scott."

Dave's father glanced past the man. "You picked a good place to stay away from the Yankees," he said quietly.

Rance flushed. He placed a hand on the butt of his pistol. "I got my duties here! I'm guardin' this ram from Yankee spies."

Dave's throat went dry. Sam Rance was well known and much hated in that country. He had served for a time in Virginia, or so he said, fighting with General Lee, but no one had ever seen proof of that fact. He spent his time riding about the country running down runaway slaves, deserters, and men who spoke openly for the Union. He and his ragtag, bobtail company of guerrillas and local scum had a notorious reputation for pig- and chicken-stealing but not for much else.

"Get down off that waggin," said Rance. "I got questions to ask yuh."

Micah Scott got down. "I'll talk to Commander Cooke," he said quietly, "but not to you, Rance."

Rance stepped forward. He cuffed Dave aside. Dave's ears rang as he fell back against the wagon.

Dave's father stepped in close. He jerked the Colt from Rance's belt and threw it into a pile of shavings. Rance threw a hard right hook toward Micah's face, but Micah Scott had been known as a first-class rough-and-tumble man in the Navy and in the Chowan River country. Micah blocked the blow with his left shoulder and hit Rance on the jaw with a short, pile-driving blow that lifted Rance

15

clean from his feet and dumped him on the ground. He reached for a sheath knife, but Micah Scott moved in close and stamped his left foot on Rance's wrist, pinning it to the ground. " Now, Sam," he said with a grin, " you wouldn't start a fight with a one-armed man, would you? "

" Fight! Fight! " a workman yelled.

Men dropped their tools and streamed toward the two men. Micah stepped back. Rance got to his feet, and there was pure hate in his dark eyes.

A dignified-looking man hurried toward the two antagonists. He wore a naval uniform. It was Commander Cooke. " Gentlemen! Gentlemen! " he called out.

Rance wiped the blood that trickled from his mouth. Dave reached into the wagon and placed his hand on a short metal bar that had not been taken with the rest of the metal.

Commander Cooke looked at Rance. " What happened? "

Rance jerked a thumb at Micah Scott. " This man ain't no loyal Confedrit. He's a Yankee-lover. I only wanted to ask him some questions, and he hit me."

" He's lying! " said Dave.

" Shut up, you! " snapped Rance.

Commander Cooke looked at Micah. " Is Captain Rance right? "

"No. The man doesn't like me. He hit my boy. I disarmed him and knocked him down. When he reached for his knife, I stepped on his arm to stop him from drawing it. That's all."

There was a look of dislike on the naval officer's face as he glanced at Rance. " This man brought metal for the ram. He came here in good faith. You had no right to annoy him, sir."

16

" I got my duties to do! "

Cooke raised his head. " I have not seen any orders detailing you to duty here, sir. You've done nothing but lounge around and make trouble."

Rance shook a fist at Micah. " Yeh, but what about him? Taking my gun, knocking me down, stepping on my arm! "

" A one-armed man, *Captain* Rance? "

The man who had shown Dave about the ram suddenly began to laugh, and in a moment every man in the crowd was roaring with laughter at the incongruous situation. An unarmed man, with but one arm, had taken a pistol away from the swaggering bully and had knocked him down with ease.

Rance shot angry looks from beneath his brows at the laughing men; then he looked at Micah Scott. " I'm leavin' here. I ain't appreciated for what I been doin' here, and I aim to go back down south. You look out for me, Yankee-lover! " He turned on a heel, retrieved his pistol, and walked toward the shanty.

Cooke waved a hand. " Back to work, men! We can't get the *Albemarle* finished this way! "

The men drifted off, and then Cooke turned to David's father. " I'm sorry, sir. Rance is a bully and a braggart." Cooke smiled. " Thanks for getting him out of my hair. I have been wondering how I could do it myself."

Dave's father got up into the wagon, followed by Dave. " Thank you sir," said Micah. He slapped the reins against the mules and drove toward the rise. He looked back as they reached the top of the rise. " She'll be ready before too long," he said quietly. " She's a veritable Goliath. What did you learn about her? "

Dave related the information he had learned from the foreman. Micah Scott smiled. " You should be a Pinkerton

17

agent," he said. " The Union Navy will be interested in your information. What do you think? "

Dave nodded. They'd be interested all right, but what could they do about it? The Union vessels in the sounds were fast and able, carrying heavy guns, but they could not stop that metal behemoth.

Micah Scott tugged at the reins. " Rance will make trouble for us soon enough. I want to get out of this country. Is that all right with you? "

" We're Union men, sir."

Dave looked back at the monster as they drove on. It would take not only vessels and guns of iron to stop her, but men of iron as well.

Chapter 2

THE SUN was low in the west when Dave pulled his little skiff alongside the rickety wharf in front of his home on the banks of the Chowan. A cold January wind swept across the choppy river and thrashed the tree branches. Dave was chilled to the bone. He moored the skiff and heaved the basket of fish up onto the wharf. The yellow light shone through the dusty windows of the house.

He had been out fishing since daylight and had gone right out into the sound. He had seen Union picket boats at a distance, for Plymouth, on the Roanoke, on the south side of the sound, was in Union hands, but there were other local fishermen out on the sound, and if they should see him talking to the Union sailors, they'd make plenty of trouble for the Scotts. Only the fact that the Denbys, Dave's mother's people, had always been well thought of in that area, had saved him and his father from much annoyance by the secessionists.

Dave was lonely; he was always lonely these days. His parents had taken him out of school shortly after the war had started over two and a half years ago. Some of the older boys in the school had called him Yankee-lover and other cutting names, and there had been a few hard-

19

fought fights. His mother and father had taught him themselves and had taught him well, and as a result he had a better education than most of the grown men in that area. He meant to go to sea some day as his father had done, and not before the mast, but as an officer or master's mate.

He opened the kitchen door and placed the fish basket inside it; then he washed himself in the bucket placed just outside the door. He drew the comb through his thick reddish hair and then went inside. His father came into the kitchen. "Davie," he said quietly, "I've sold the house at last."

The cold searching wind moaned about the eaves and rattled the windows. A shutter banged against the side of the house. The oil lamp guttered in the strong draft.

"I had to, Davie," said Micah Scott. "Your mother always seems to be here still. I couldn't have stood it much longer."

Dave nodded. His mother's invisible presence seemed to linger in the old house where she had been born and raised.

"There are only the two of us now, Davie."

"Where shall we go, Father?"

Micah Scott placed a huge wad of crumpled Confederate bills on the table. "This looks like a great deal of money, but it's hardly worth the paper it's printed upon. I gave your mother my word that I would not take up arms against the Confederacy while she was still alive, but I think she understood I would go north when she was gone."

Dave looked at his father's empty left sleeve.

Micah nodded as if he understood what Dave was thinking. "I know these coastal waters better than most men. I need only one arm to be a pilot."

"I know that!" said Dave quickly.

"There are blockade-runners leaving Wilmington almost every day, Dave. They always need good seamen, and more than seamen they need good pilots. They pay well — in gold. We need that money. I can't return to the Navy and leave you penniless in some northern city. We can work our way to the Bahamas or perhaps to Halifax, in Nova Scotia, and take ship from there to New York or Boston. What do you say?"

Dave smiled. "I'm a Yankee too, sir!"

~

There was a slow drizzle of rain descending on Wilmington as Dave Scott walked along the teeming river front while killing time waiting for his father, who was trying to ship aboard a blockade-runner. The river was full of slim-hulled blockade-runners, anchored in the stream or made fast to the sagging wharves. Across the river he could hear the noise of the big steam presses as they formed bales of cotton. The wharves and warehouses were packed with cotton, tobacco, and barrels of turpentine, all prime outward-bound cargoes. Some of the runners were already loaded with bales of cotton covering the decks in several layers, leaving just enough room to enter the cabins, the forecastle, and the engine room. A crew of men was hard at work, using big screw jacks to compress the bales still further for closer packing on the decks and in the holds.

The blockade-runners would slip down the stream to Smithville and wait for the high tide over the bar to start their runs for Nassau in the Bahamas, Bermuda, or Halifax, which were the main cotton-receiving ports for eventual transshipment to the cotton-hungry mills of England.

The South was in dire need of opium, quinine, calomel, and other medicaments. The rebel armies needed rifles, caps, lead, powder, artillery pieces, and other military equipment. They needed uniforms, shoes, blankets, tents, and other impedimenta. Dave had heard it said that two million people in England were on the brink of starvation because of the loss of cotton for the mills. It was a highly profitable trade for the blockade-runners, for such items as quinine could be bought at two dollars and eighty cents an ounce in Nassau and sold in rebel ports for twelve hundred dollars an ounce. Currency could buy, at ten cents a pound, cotton that in Nassau was sold for fifty cents a pound in gold specie.

Dave had also heard it said that the rebel armies marched on English-tanned leather, wore English-made uniforms, and were largely fed on Cincinnati bacon and corned beef shipped to Nassau by Northern speculators and thence carried into rebel ports by the daring blockade-runners. Most of the runners had been built in England, and were skippered by English captains and crewed by English and Scottish packet rats. Indeed, a great many of the runners were owned by British companies, and the greatest of these was Alexander Collie Company of Glasgow.

It was necessary to give two thousand dollars in Confederate money for one dollar of specie in Wilmington. Dave's father had priced wearing apparel the first day they had been in the port and had been aghast at the costs. A pair of man's boots cost five hundred dollars while a suit of shoddy cost six hundred dollars. An overcoat of poor material cost fifteen hundred dollars. A ham cost fifty dollars, a barrel of flour was worth five hundred dollars, and tea and coffee cost one hundred dollars a pound.

But the blockade-running sailors lived high on the hog because they were paid in gold. Most of them were from Bristol, Liverpool, Milford Haven, and Cardiff, with a sprinkling of Scots and Tynesiders. Micah Scott had told Dave that many of the captains and crews were former members of the Royal Navy, some of them on leave with the blessing of the Admiralty, for the British needed cotton to save their economy. Dave had seen many of the sailors swaggering about town, with gold hoops in their ears and expensive silk scarves about their brown necks, throwing money around with prodigal hands.

But the blockade-runners had brought more than supplies and money into Wilmington. In the summer of 1862 they had brought yellow jack, and before the plague was stamped out, more than a third of the six thousand people of Wilmington had died of the disease.

Dave leaned against a bollard on a wharf and watched with curiosity a lean, buff-colored steamer that was moored, with steam up, in the stream. Her decks were piled high with cotton. Dave saw smoke drifting from the hatches and from the ventilators. A British sailor walked past Dave with a seaman's rolling walk. " Is she on fire? " asked Dave.

The seaman turned quickly. " The *Whisper*, lad? No. 'Tis the provost and his crew smoking out the holds."

" To kill rats? "

The man laughed. " No! The provost thinks there is a deserter stowed away below." He eyed Dave. " Ye're new here? "

"Yes."

The sailor lighted a cigar and puffed it into life. "I've made several trips into here. Every return voyage is slowed down by that scum of a provost poking about looking for deserters. Poor lads. They haven't a chance with that smoke filling the holds. Watch, lad, and ye'll see soon enough."

There were armed men on the decks of the *Whisper,* clad in ill-fitting, butternut-colored uniforms, leaning on their rifles. A lean man paced back and forth, peering at the companionways with a hunter's interest. There was something familiar about him. Then Dave saw the bedraggled feather on the man's wet hat and knew it was Cap'n Sam Rance. "Rance!" said Dave.

"Ye know him?" asked the sailor.

"Yes."

"Scum! Last voyage I saw him catch a deserter. He picked the man clean before he took him to the jail. Just a boy he was, hardly older than ye. It made me blood boil to see the lad mistreated by that uniformed jackal."

There was a shout from Rance. A man had appeared at a doorway, gagging and coughing, blackened by smoke. Rance whipped out his pistol and smashed the heavy barrel against the side of the deserter's head, driving him to the deck. He booted him twice and then jerked his head at his men. He picked up the unconscious prisoner and hurled him over the rail into a waiting boat. Dave looked away.

"Aye, 'tis hard on them," said the sailor.

The boat was pulled toward the wharf. Dave stepped behind a pile of cotton bales. He watched the provost drag the man to the wharf and throw him into a two-wheeled cart. Rance swaggered about as though he had just taken a Federal gun battery by storm.

Dave turned to slip away, but the sailor gripped him by the arm. " Ye looking for a berth, lad? I'm bosun on the *Wave Queen,* and we can use a bright lad like ye for cabin boy. Pays well."

" I have to go."

" Fifty pounds a month sterling. Ye can hardly overlook that."

Rance was close to Dave now. Dave wrenched himself free and ran for the street.

" Wait, you! " yelled Cap'n Rance.

Dave sprinted down the street, dodging wagons and pedestrians.

" That boy's a deserter! " yelled Rance.

Dave darted into a filthy alleyway and sprinted for all he was worth. He slipped in the greasy mud and went down. Rance appeared at the end of the alley. Dave got to his feet and raced for the next street. A familiar figure walked toward him. It was his father.

" What's wrong, David? " asked Micah.

" It's Cap'n Rance! " gasped Dave. " He's provost."

Micah gripped Dave by the arm and ran him toward a warehouse. They jumped inside and ran to the back of it. Boots thudded in the alley.

Micah tried the rear door, but it was locked. He pushed Dave behind some barrels. " Quiet! " he snapped.

Boots grated on the floor of the warehouse. Micah closed his right hand. Rance appeared, blinking in the semi-darkness. Micah stepped forward and smashed a fist against the provost's jaw, driving him back against a post. Rance drew his Colt and slammed it against Micah's head. Dave's father went down. Rance grinned as he cocked the heavy Colt.

Dave snatched up a thick billet of wood. He darted out and threw it at Rance. " You! " yelled the provost just as the billet caught him flush on the jaw. He went down, rolled over, and lay still.

Micah got to his feet. " Let's go," he said. " I got a berth on the runner *Phantom,* now in the stream down at Smithville, waiting to leave for Halifax. Her pilot died three days ago of yellow jack. I hired a boat to take us down. We have to hurry. They want to catch the eleven o'clock high water."

They hurried out into the street. Three of the provost's men stood at the end of the street looking the other way. Micah and Dave darted into an alley and walked toward the river. A boat was moored to a wharf, and two powerful-looking Negroes rested on the oars. Dave dropped into the boat and his father followed him. " Take the tiller," said Micah to Dave. He felt inside his coat. " Rance won't keep us here," he said quietly. Micah drew out a pistol. " Cast off," he said. " Row as hard as you can."

" Yes, boss," said one of the Negroes. His eyes were wide in his head as he shoved the boat out into the stream. Dave took the tiller and looked back. There were soldiers walking toward the wharf. He steered the swiftly moving boat close to the gray hull of a runner, out of sight of the provost's men.

Micah Scott felt his bruised head. " Close, that one," he said, smiling. " Thanks, Davie."

The rain came down heavily as they passed the bow of the runner. It was more than twenty miles down the Cape Fear River to Smithville, point of departure for the blockade-runners.

Chapter 3

THE BLOCKADE-RUNNER *Phanthom* tugged uneasily at her anchor chain where she lay in the Cape Fear River just off Smithville. Mists drifted down the wide river, and there was a spit of rain in the cold air.

Dave stood on the deck outside the little cabin that had been assigned to his father. The water lapped against the thin steel hull of the runner. Now and then he could hear the scraping of a stoker's coal scoop on the iron plates of the engine room below as the black gang got up a head of steam.

Micah Scott came along the deck and stopped beside Dave. " It won't be long now," he said. " Excited? "

" Yes! "

" We'll leave in a little while. The picket boats are due back soon, and then we'll know if we can slip past the blockaders. We haven't decided as yet whether to leave by New Inlet or through the Western Bar Channel. We'll probably take the Western Bar Channel."

" Aren't both channels guarded by rebel forts? "

" Yes. Fort Fisher near New Inlet; Fort Caswell just below us here. The blockaders usually stay beyond range of the cannons at the forts. I've heard that Fort Fisher has English Whitworth guns which can throw a shell five miles at angles of twenty-five degrees. They've made quite a few hits on the blockaders."

" They can't see them at night, though."

" No. It's then that the Federals move their ships in close. They put out their lights and anchor just off the inlets. They form a sort of floating box out there, allowing just enough room for a blockade-runner to pass through into the box, and then shoot off Coston flares to light up the runner. Then it's grape, solid shot, and canister coming in from three sides, with the beach on the fourth side. Some captains prefer the beach to surrendering. They tell me the beaches are cluttered with wrecked and burned runners."

Dave swallowed hard.

" Scared? " asked his father.

" No! "

" Well . . . *I* am," said Micah Scott, dryly.

" The steward told me the Union seamen raid right up the river, sometimes almost as far as Wilmington."

" Yes. They have a young daredevil out there in command of a fast screw steamer named the *Monticello*. Just a short time ago he penetrated this river with a gig and a cutter, manned by only twenty men.

" They got past Fort Caswell all right and Bald Head too, without being seen, until they were northeast of Smithville. They came down-river then, as though they were rebel pickets, and landed right in the town.

" Cushing, that's the name of the *Monticello*'s commander, went ashore with four or five men, in an attempt to capture General Hébert and take him out of town by means of a captured steamer, but there weren't any steamers here at the time.

"Cushing had the brassbound nerve to go right to the general's house, past the barracks of the rebel troops, only fifty yards away. But Hébert, by ill fortune, had gone up to Wilmington, and so Cushing captured Captain Kelly, chief engineer of the port defenses, and then managed to get away.

"They slipped down the river past Fort Caswell again, hearing the drums playing the long roll to alert the troops. They made it safely to their ship.

"Later, Cushing sent a note to Fort Caswell regretting that Hébert wasn't at home when he had called."

Dave grinned. "I'd like to meet that man Cushing."

"With men like him in the blockading fleet, we haven't much to fear about the vaunted boastings of rebel superiority. Even Colonel Jones, commandant of Fort Caswell, was amused by Cushing's daring and impudence. The result of the whole escapade was a strengthening of the river defenses. Cushing received a roving commission in order to cruise out beyond the line of blockading vessels to catch inbound and outbound blockade-runners."

A seaman came down the deck and knuckled his forehead. "Captain Stewart's compliments, sir," he said, "and he'd like to see ye on the bridge. 'Tis almost time to drop down the river, sir."

Micah walked toward the low bridge. Dave walked forward to where he could see the yellow lights of Smithville dimly through the wet mist.

The *Phantom* was a racer, built in Leeds, England, and owned by Alexander Collie Company of Glasgow. She had a slender hull and outsized paddle wheels in huge housings. There was a turtleback covering over her bow, extending almost to the low superstructure. She had two short, raked masts without topmasts or cross yards. She had two slim, raked funnels which could be telescoped to shorten them. Thin wraiths of smoke drifted from them, and the air filled with the tang of Welsh coal.

Dave walked about the decks, threading his way through the aisles left between the stacked bales of cotton. The vessel had been painted completely in light gray and had a minimum of superstructure and long, sweeping lines. Even as she lay at anchor she gave the impression of the great speed of which she was capable, for she could do fourteen knots with good anthracite feeding her boiler fires. Most of her two-hundred-foot deck was packed with cotton bales.

A hoarse command rang out from the bridge. Seamen wearing slippers or in their bare feet began to rig tarpaulins over fireroom hatches, ventilators, and companionways to exclude lights and noises. The boats had already been lowered to the decks to cut down the dim silhouette of the *Phantom*. The seamen wore white clothing, as dark clothing could be seen too easily against the light paint of the superstructure. Lookouts scurried up the shrouds to take their posts. They were paid a dollar for every sail or thread of smoke they spotted and fined five dollars if a deckman saw it first. Other sharp-eyed lookouts took their posts at the bow, on the bridge, on the paddle-wheel boxes, and on the quarter-deck.

Dave heard the muffled ringing of coal scoops on the fireroom deck plates. The anchor was hove up short, then catted. The current caught the slender hull as the paddle wheels began to turn. Smoke drifted from the two slender funnels. The lights of Smithville came up abeam and then drifted astern.

The great paddle wheels churned the salty waters into foam. There was a rhythmic coughing of steam from the exhausts. The water curled back from the knifelike prow. The *Phantom* was one of many such vessels engaged in a dangerous trade. Such an enterprise was a gamble with immense profits to the gained. They had losses too, those swift, elusive craft. Many lay wrecked off Cape Fear.

Dave had heard the blockade-running seamen laughing at the Federal Navy's " soapbox " blockade, composed of former merchant vessels, ferryboats, tugs, double-enders, and other mongrel craft, few of which could catch a swift runner like the *Phantom*. Still, as the *Phantom* slipped down the channel, Dave looked through the clinging mist and gentle rain, and felt a touch of fear within him. If men like Cushing could penetrate the stout defenses of the Cape Fear River and land in a town where a thousand rebel soldiers were stationed, they would also have enough courage and skill to stop such racers as the *Phantom*. There was no protection against the heavily shotted guns of the blockaders, and even if the runners had been armed, they would be treated like pirates for firing back. They relied solely on speed and their light coloring to escape.

A man hailed the *Phantom* from the darkness of the river and was answered from the bridge. A little steamer drifted past the vessel, and the decks held men in butter-nut-colored uniforms, carrying brightly polished rifles. The rebel flag flew from the taffrail. In a moment she had been swallowed by the clinging mist.

Dave went up the ladder to the bridge and peered inside. A brawny quartermaster held the wheel, peering

31

into a funnel-like canvas cover that masked the binnacle light. It was the only light aboard beyond that of the fireboxes in the engine room. Micah Scott stood beside the helmsman, his face drawn as he peered through the wet glass before him. Red-faced Captain Donald Stewart stood behind Micah, and there was a worried look about him.

Beyond Cape Fear were the treacherous Frying Pan Shoals, notorious and dangerous, which stretched ten miles out into the Atlantic. In the channel ahead of them was " the Lump," a small sandy knoll three miles off the bar with plenty of deep water on each side of it, but the night was dark enough for even a skilled pilot like Micah Scott to be uncertain as to exactly where he was.

Dave went down to the deck and out forward of the bridge just behind the turtleback. He saw dim blue lights to starboard and figured they must be from Fort Caswell. The *Phantom* was surging and swaying as she met a stronger current. Spindrift flew back from the cleaving bow as the *Phantom* met quick surges of the sea.

They must be close to the bar now, thought Dave. He turned up his collar against the wet searching wind and peered into the darkness.

He seemed to see shadowy shapes beyond the bow. The faint slapping of the paddles and the vibration of the hull mingled with the rushing noise of the bow wash. It seemed as if the pale waters were rougher. The *Phantom* pitched and shook. There was a faint rushing noise from beneath the thin hull, and then the *Phantom* seemed to ring like a dropped tin pan as she surged across the unseen bar. The shore loom to starboard was dimly visible now as the wind shifted to part the mist. The channel mouth was more than a half a mile wide, but Dave thought he heard the faint roaring of the surf against Smith Island to port.

There were freakish tidal flows in those waters, and it was difficult enough to gauge them during daylight. At night, in the mist, it was almost like a game of blindman's buff.

The hull began to quiver more strongly with the increased thrusting of the paddle wheels. The vessel had a draft of ten or twelve feet with too narrow a hull, and she began to roll sickeningly in the swells. Soon they would have to start the pumps, for such vessels, built as they were, leaked a great deal.

The frash-frash-frash of the paddles increased. Dave stared into the murk. He thought he saw something white just ahead of the *Phantom*. It seemed to be a large cutter with a crew of dark-clad men in it. He made out the dim glistening of the wet oars as the men pulled desperately to get out of the path of the speeding blockade-runner. Dave opened his mouth to yell and thought better of it. His voice would be heard for a great distance.

Suddenly the cutter seemed to be right under the knife-like prow. A man yelled from the cutter. There was a crashing noise as the runner sheered off the tough ash oars, hurling men against each other and into the bottom of the heaving boat. Dave stared over the low rail as the cutter swept past. A gun cracked flatly from the boat. Then the boat was astern. A moment later a rocket shot up from it to trace a crazy wavering course against the night sky.

Dave looked up to see dim blue lights in the distance, and he could make out the tall masts of a dark vessel not two hundred yards from the racing *Phantom*. Another rocket sailed up high into the sky. Coston flares burst into light, and Dave saw two more vessels just beyond the first one he had seen. A gun flashed and thundered.

The *Phantom* heeled hard astarboard as the darkness seemed to come alive with soaring rockets and crashing guns. She followed the surf line, just off shore, with the hiss and pound of her engines timed with the thrashing of the huge paddle wheels. The wind seemed to moan through the rigging and about the superstructure.

Dave heard again the hiss and sucking of the sand against the bottom of the hull. The vessel hit hard and rang like a church bell, and then she turned to sea again with a veil of mist between her and the blockaders.

A seaman grinned at Dave as he walked past. " 'Tis all over now, me lad, and ye'll be in Halifax before too long. We've given the Yankees the slip again. Heigh-ho! "

Dave began to breathe easier. He had always felt at home while at sea, for he had been born with salt water in his veins, but this type of business was a little too risky to suit him.

He padded aft and entered his cabin. He dropped onto the bunk without undressing and lay there staring up into the darkness, feeling the sickening lift and sway of the fragile hull as the *Phantom* rushed toward the open sea.

Chapter 4

DAVE opened his eyes with a start as the *Phantom* made a particularly vicious pitch followed by a snap roll. The slender hull seemed to spring upward as though propelled from below, and Dave flew out of his bunk like a great ungainly bird and crashed onto the deck. Pale light showed through the porthole. The engines were driving at full speed, and the straining hull was vibrating and throbbing violently. He pulled himself to his feet, thankful for no broken bones.

Above the pounding of the engines he heard a dull thudding noise. He put on his cap and clawed his way up the sloping deck to the door to grip the handle. Even as he gripped it, to open it, the door swung outward as the vessel made its return roll, and he was hurled clear across the deck to end up with a crash against the gunwale. Spray shot over the rail and doused him. He came up spluttering and heard again the dull thudding noise. Then something seemed to whisper over the *Phantom*.

He pulled himself to his feet. A seaman hurried past him. " Yankee blockader! " he yelled. " A fast one too! That last shot was a close one! Did ye hear it whisper of death as it passed between the funnels?"

Dave felt a little sick. That had been the rushing noise he had heard. He looked to port. Two slender masts showed above a deep trough in the heaving waves, and even as he looked he saw a sharp bowsprit poke up, followed by a lean black hull. There was a flash and puff of smoke from the blockader, followed by a dull explosion. A cannon ball appeared magically and skipped from wave crest to wave crest only to plunge out of sight beneath the water fifty feet from the bow of the runner.

The steward appeared beside Dave. "She's fast, that one," he said in his Scots burr, "and carrying full sail along wi' her steam power, and in this half a gale too."

"Will she catch us?"

"Her? Catch the *Phantom*? Never a chance, laddie. It's thae guns that might mak the difference. How they can shoot sae well in this broth of a sea and wi' this wind, is beyond me. One ball through a boiler and we'll blow up intae scrap metal!"

The steward wiped the spray from his bearded face. "Anither hour o' darkness and we'd hae made it. Now it's a stern chase and it will be a lang one."

The blockader rode low in the water, and she had fast, trim lines. She was brigantine-rigged, with fore-and-aft sails on her mainmast and square sails on her foremast. She had one slender funnel from which streamed dark smoke.

"Aboot seven hundred ton, I'd say," said the steward.

The *Phantom* had the edge on the blockader as far as speed went, but she was making heavy weather of it, plunging into the rough seas while thick water flowed over the turtleback and poured along her decks. The

36

pumps were pounding steadily as she fought to keep the water down in her fragile hull.

A guy wire snapped like a violin string. Water surged knee-deep past Dave and the steward. The blockader fired again as the blockade-runner turned into the eye of the wind to deprive the pursuing vessel the advantage of her sails. Splinters flew and the steward dropped to the deck. Something clanged against one of the funnels. Dave turned to see a gaping hole where his cabin had been. He could see clear through to the starboard deck. He swallowed hard. Much as he wanted the blockader to run down the *Phantom*, he now wished the straining *Phantom* would drain all the speed she could from her racing engines.

The steward stood up and placed his mouth close to Dave's ear. " If she catches us, we'll spend the rest of the war at Fort Lafayette or Fort Warren eating rats and hardtack. They'll never let yere fayther go, lad, because pilots are considered tae be too valuable to exchange."

The *Phantom* seemed to groan in agony as she plunged deeply and then rose sluggishly to meet the next sea.

" Fog bank three miles ahead," said the steward. " Pilot is makin' for it."

Dave had forgotten about his father. Now he clawed his way along the streaming deck until he reached the bridge ladder. The bow dived down, and there was a thundering crash of green water on the turtleback. He looked over his shoulder to see tons of water, flecked with white foam, bearing down on him.

" Davie! Davie! Davie! " yelled his father from the bridge.

It was the last thing he heard as the water picked him up like a chip and carried him aft past the paddle-wheel housing. The water flowed past, and for a moment he saw his father leaning from the bridge door and staring at him with a set, white face. Then another graybeard of a wave picked David up neatly and flowed with him right over the side, past the thrashing steel paddles. He went down deep into the cold water.

He ripped off his shoes and shrugged out of his heavy pea jacket. His breath was going fast, and there was a mortal fear in him that he'd come up beneath the paddles. He swam down and then outward with all his might until he could bear it no longer. He surfaced to see the slim stern of the *Phantom* a good hundred yards ahead of him, and then he went under again.

He slid off his heavy trousers as he surfaced again. He was a strong swimmer, but little good it would do him now. He saw a man hurl something over the stern. It rose high on a wave and flowed toward him. Dave began to swim slowly and steadily toward the object, conserving his strength. He heard the dull thudding of the blockader's guns now and then, but the *Phantom* was too far away from him by now for him to see if she had been hit again.

Dave looked over his shoulder. He was almost right in the course of the blockader, but she was more than a mile from him. The *Phantom* was swifter all right.

He reached the object that had been thrown overboard. It was a wooden grating, hardly enough to keep him afloat, but it was better than swimming. He rested on it. The *Phantom* was almost to the fog bank by now, and she was out of range too. The blockader fired another gun in rage and frustration just as the tattered fog bank seemed to swallow the *Phantom*.

The fog was drifting toward Dave. It might envelop

him before the Union ship found him. He was cold enough from the water, but now the cold of fear settled in his body and mind. If the blockader passed him in the fog, there wasn't a chance for him to survive on the lonely tossing waters.

A shower of spray flew back from the bow of the trim Union vessel. She was still making knots toward the fog bank like a bulldog determined to come to grips with her foe. Dave could see the intricate curling design that had been picked out on the bow in gold paint. She was a beauty, low and trim, more like a yacht than a man-of-war.

The wind snapped out her flag, and it gave Dave a thrill, cold as he was, to see the Stars and Stripes once more. He could see men moving about on her wet decks as she pitched and rolled with a bone in her teeth. Her white sails seemed carved from marble so taut were they.

She was only a few hundred yards from Dave now. He waved an arm and yelled, but all he got for his pains was a dollop of salt water into his mouth and he spluttered into silence.

The dark hull seemed to tower over him, and he yelled again. He paddled frantically to get away from the sharp cutwater. A sailor yelled from the deck, and another raced up the foreshrouds to look at him. He yelled too and pointed down toward Dave. The bow dipped deeply, showering back spray, and Dave saw the name of the vessel amidst the gold curlicues. It was the *Monticello*. He seemed to remember vaguely hearing about that vessel.

A man looked over the rail of the quarter-deck. " It's just a boy! " he yelled. He cupped his hands about his mouth. " Stand by to come about! "

Dave lost his grip on the grating as the wave made by

the passage of the fast vessel flowed over him. He went down and then bobbed up again. The man who had given the commands ripped off his officer's cap and long frock coat. With his long hair blowing in the wind, he climbed to the rail and then dived cleanly into the water with hardly a splash.

The head bobbed up a few feet away from David, and he found himself looking into a bony face plastered with wet brown hair. The officer swam to Dave and held him up, treading water easily. His calm eyes studied Dave. "Take it easy," he said. "It's a nice day for a swim."

His voice gave Dave new courage. The *Monticello* had turned into the wind, and the sails were fluttering and slatting about as the powerful screw bit into the water and drove the vessel toward the two swimmers.

"What ship was that you were on?" asked Dave's companion.

"The *Phantom.*"

A wry look passed across the officer's face. "She's well named. Did we get any hits?"

"One through the cabins. There might have been others. I left her in too much of a hurry to notice any more."

"We have first-class gunners aboard the *Monticello.* Getting a hit at that range and in this sea is first-class shooting."

The blockader was close to them now. Seamen were taking in sail as the screw went into reverse and slowed the way of the ship. A heaving line shot out from the deck, and the plaited knot at the end of it struck Dave on the head. He grabbed it and felt himself being pulled toward the craft. A Jacob's ladder was heaved over the side, and he gripped it as the vessel rose on a swell. He reached

40

the rail, and strong hands pulled him to the deck. " There ye be, all shipshape and Bristol fashion," said a hearty voice.

The officer followed Dave to the deck. " Take him to the galley and warm him up inside and outside," he said. " Dry clothing and a hot drink. Jump and make it so, Scrimshaw."

The seaman knuckled his forehead. " Aye, aye, sir! "

Dave eyed the sailor. He saw a broad, good-humored face framed in salt-and-pepper-colored chin whiskers. " Come ye with me, rebel," said Scrimshaw. There was a strong New England accent to his voice.

Seamen and gunners stared at Dave. A young sailor, about Dave's age, with a magnificently freckled face, stuck his hand below his chin and waggled it at Dave. " Fort Lafayette for you, blockade-runner," he said.

" Stow your gab, Steve Raintree," said a gunner. " The lad is chilled to the bone."

The crew were all rugged-looking men with tanned faces, wearing broad, flat hats and loose-fitting blues. The vessel was as neat and trim from a deck view as she had been from a sea view. Dave was hustled to the galley and inside it. He was grateful to get away from the cutting wind.

A huge Negro clucked his tongue in sympathy as he saw Dave shivering. He stirred a huge copper pot. " Pore little man," he said in a deep voice. " Ol' Ginger fix you up. We got good navy beans for breakus."

The pungent odor of the beans made Dave realize he had not eaten since the late afternoon of the day before. Scrimshaw stepped back and squinted at Dave. " I'll raid the slop chest. We'll rig ye out in honest Union blue, rebel."

"I'm not a rebel," said Dave quickly. "My father is as good a Union man as you, sailor."

"So? And ye on a blockade-runner?"

"I can explain that."

Ginger grinned. "I'll jes bet he kin too, Scrimshaw."

Scrimshaw shrugged. "Ye're liable to find anything in this ocean from sea sarpents to mermaids." He left the galley and slid the door shut.

"Git outta them wet drawers, boy," said Ginger, "else you'll get your death of cold."

Dave stripped himself, and Ginger handed him a big apron to cover himself. The cook ladled some beans into a bowl and handed the bowl to Dave. "Dive in, son. You had a close call, little massa. Old Davy Jones nearly got his cold, wet hands on you."

Dave ate the luscious beans and then smiled at Ginger. "Thanks," he said.

"No bother."

Scrimshaw entered the galley with an armload of clothing. "Get into these duds, boy, and jump to it. The skipper wants to see ye aft."

Dave pulled on warm drawers and a pair of floppy pants. He shrugged into the loose middy blouse and placed a flat hat on his head. There were no shoes, and he had noticed that neither Scrimshaw nor Ginger wore any. They weren't much good on a wet, heaving deck.

"Ye have the right cut to yere jib for a seagoing man," said the sailor.

"My father is a seagoing man," said Dave.

Scrimshaw grinned. "Aye, I would have thought so." He took Dave by the arm. "The skipper is waiting."

"Who was that officer who jumped in to help me?"

Ginger waved a hand. "*That* was the skipper, son."

42

" He left his ship to save me? "

Scrimshaw nodded. " Ye'll know what manner of man he is after ye get to know him better."

" But he's so young to be the skipper of a man-of-war! "

" Aye, he's young in years, 'tis true, but more of a man at twenty-one years of age than many a skipper twice that age."

" Who is he? "

Scrimshaw raised his head proudly. " Lieutenant William Barker Cushing, U.S.N., commanding the U.S.S. *Monticello!* "

Dave remembered the story his father had told him the night before on the *Phantom*. Cushing! The young daredevil who had almost captured General Hébert!

" Jump and show a leg! " said Scrimshaw. " Smartly now! "

They walked aft along the heaving deck which had been holystoned to almost a pure white. The vessel was neat and shipshape, with gleaming brass and taut rigging.

The sailor led the way down a ladder and along a companionway until he reached the last door in a row of doors. He rapped on it, slid it open, and knuckled his forehead. " Captain Cushing, sir, here is the lad."

Cushing was over six feet tall, of slender but wiry build, and weighed about one hundred and fifty pounds. He was drying his long hair with a towel. " You're all right now, lad? " he asked.

" Yes, sir."

" Your name? "

" David Denby Scott, sir."

" Where are you from? "

" I was born in Baltimore, sir, but I've lived most of my life on the Chowan River in North Carolina."

There was the faintest ghost of a smile on Cushing's face. "A rebel?"

"No, sir!"

"He said his father was as good a Union man as myself, sir," said Scrimshaw.

"Then he must be a good Union man indeed! Sit down, David, and tell me all about yourself."

Dave sat down on a chair and told the story of how he had happened to be aboard the *Phantom.*

Cushing paced back and forth. "You say your father wanted to go to Halifax in order to get a ship to take him to New York or Boston so that he might join our Navy?"

"Yes, sir."

The steady eyes held David's. "The war started three years ago. How is it that he did not leave North Carolina before now?"

Dave explained the loss of the *Alice* and how his father had been disabled; then he went on to tell of how his mother's lingering illness had kept his father at home. He watched Cushing as the young officer looked out of a porthole. "If you don't believe that my father and I are Union men, sir, I can tell you what we learned about the rebel ram *Albemarle.*"

Cushing whirled and his eyes seemed to light up. "*What do you know about that ram?*"

"I've seen her and have even been aboard her, sir."

"Tell me everything you know about her. *Everything!*"

Both men listened intently as Dave told all he knew about the powerful ram.

Cushing looked at Scrimshaw when Dave had finished his story. "Then the rumors we have heard are true enough."

Scrimshaw nodded. "It'll be our job, sir, to stop her if we can."

Cushing shook his head. "We have no vessel powerful enough to face her in the sounds. It would take a cutting-out expedition to get her."

Scrimshaw grinned widely. "I know what the Captain is thinking about that too."

Cushing smashed his right fist into his left palm. "It should be *my* job! Who else could do it?"

"No one, sir, with the possible exception of Commander Rowan, sir."

Cushing flushed. "Yes . . . he ranks me, sure enough."

Scrimshaw tilted his head to one side. "But *will* he do it, Captain?"

"I hope not."

Cushing paced back and forth as if his agile mind was already conceiving a plan to destroy the ram. He stopped and looked at Dave. "You'll have to stay aboard until we go into Beaufort for supplies. I can drop you at Roanoke Island if you like."

Dave stood up. "Begging the Captain's pardon, sir, but I did not run the blockade to sit ashore."

Cushing smiled. "Well said, lad! Scrimshaw, I place this boy in your care. I saved him from the sea and it seems as if it is up to me to take care of him now. Find him a place to swing his hammock. Have him outfitted at my expense."

Dave knuckled his forehead as he had seen Scrimshaw do. "I don't want to sit around, sir. I'm no idler. I've been to sea and can hand, reef, and steer. Can't I do something aboard the *Monticello*?"

Cushing threw back his head and laughed. "Certainly!

We need a cabin boy. The last one jumped ship."

"I'll serve, sir."

Scrimshaw opened the door. "I'll take him under my wing, Captain."

They left the cabin and went up on deck. The ship was making heavy weather of it. Scrimshaw looked aloft. "Rough," he said.

"Will we run for shelter?"

"Not on the blockade, lad! We stay at sea in fair or foul weather."

The fog had blown away. There was nothing to see but a vast expanse of heaving, lead-colored water, with not another ship in sight. Dave looked to the northeast. The *Phantom* was gone and so was his father, and he wondered if his father thought of him as having drowned.

A young officer came toward them. "It seems as if we have a new recruit," he said with a smile as he eyed Dave.

"Not yet, Mister Howorth," said Scrimshaw. Scrimshaw waited until the officer passed them, and then he leaned close to Dave. "That's Ensign Howorth, one of Captain Cushing's right-hand men. He's just as keen as Cushing is to get a crack at the *Albemarle*."

Dave looked away. A feeling of utter loneliness had crept over him. He had always been with his father, and more so in the past years because of their pro-Union feeling which had left them pretty much alone in the Chowan River country. He knew his father was safe, so it wasn't so bad for him, but his father would suffer a great deal until he found Dave again.

Chapter 5

D o you hear the news there, sleepers?"
The loud voice of Jimmylegs, the master-at-arms,
cut through the veil of sleep about Dave. He opened his
eyes and saw the deck beam inches above his head. His
hammock swung steadily back and forth with the surging
motion of the ship.

Jimmylegs rattled his billy against the side of the ladder.
"Larbolins, ahoy! Eight bells there below! Tumble up, my
lively hearties! Steamboat alongside waiting for your
trunks! Bear a hand there, bear a hand with your trousers!
Bear a hand, my sweet and pleasant fellows! Fine shower
bath up here on deck! Hurrah! Hurrah!"

Scrimshaw thrust a sleepy face from beneath his blanket.
His hammock swung next to Dave's. "You feel sweet,
don't you, Jimmylegs?" he growled.

"Arise, you grizzly bears and growlers!" roared the im-
placable Jimmylegs.

The blockader surged and pitched, making heavy
weather of it. It was four in the morning, the beginning
of the morning watch. "Growl you may, but go you
must!" howled the master-at-arms.

"Who wouldn't sell a farm and go to sea?" asked Scrimshaw bitterly.

Dave dropped to the heaving deck and pulled on his damp uniform. He had been aboard the *Monticello* for two weeks now, standing watch with Scrimshaw and the others of the port watch. This April weather was rough and dirty off the North Carolina coast. In all that time they had not sighted another blockade-runner, but only the distant topsails of other blockaders or an occasional thread of faint smoke raveled by the strong winds.

"Oilskins today," said Frank Richmond. "It's spitting weather again."

Dave snatched up his oilskins and put them on. He hurried toward the companionway and up the ladder to the deck. Cold fingers of rain touched his face and helped awaken him fully. He looked aloft first, as all good sailors do upon reaching the deck. The *Monticello* surged along under reefed topsails, and the canvas looked as hard as marble. Water flowed along the lee rail as the gunboat drank deeply of the gray-green waves.

Scrimshaw poked his head out of the companionway and scowled. He came up on deck followed by the grumbling members of the watch. He looked aloft. "If the Bermudas let you pass," he sang out, "then beware of Hatteras!" He looked to windward. "See ye the stars, lad? See how they flicker against the dark sky? Rain or snow will follow soon."

"It's raining now," said Dave.

"Just a spit. Mark my words, it'll get worse."

"Winds in the morning, sailors take warning," said Taffy Brown as he buttoned his oilskins.

Scrimshaw looked aft. "'Tis getting cold," he said. "Fire will freeze before this day is out. But the old *Monticello* is all a-taunto. The wind's increasing. There's a fresh hand at the bellows."

"Go below the watch!" roared the boatswain.

The off watch streamed past the new watch, eager to seek the slightly comparative warmth of the berth deck.

"Man the pumps!" roared the bosun.

Scrimshaw shrugged. "'Tis ever thus. Lad, get ye to the galley for a mug-up of jamoke."

Dave walked to the galley. He wasn't really a member of the watch, but he worked with them for the experience it gave him. He was known as an idler, or one who, being at work all day, does not keep watch at night. His duties as cabin boy kept him busy enough, but he didn't intend to waste his time at sea serving officers and helping in the galley when he could gain added skill as a seaman.

Ginger was in the galley hovering over the huge pot of coffee. He handed Dave a cup. "Hungry, boy?" he asked.

"I'm always hungry," said Dave.

"They's some cut-and-come-again over there."

Dave helped himself to hard bread and cold beans, known as cut-and-come-again, food left on the table for the convenience of the crew. When he had finished eating, Ginger handed him a jug of coffee. "Jamoke for the skipper, boy," he said.

"He's up?"

"Yup. We ain't sighted a smokejack since we lost the *Phantom*, and he ain't too happy about it."

Dave took the jug and stepped out on deck. The wind caught at him and drove him reeling down the deck. He plunged down the companionway, grateful for shelter from the gale. He rapped on Cushing's door and then slid it open, knuckling his forehead as he stepped in. "Blowing half a gale, sir. The stars are flickering. Rain or snow will follow."

Cushing grinned. "I see you've been learning some of

Scrimshaw Appleby's lore." He put on his oilskins and southwester. "Scrimshaw is a sure enough stick-and-string sailor. Born and raised on sailing ships, or so he claims. Whaler, fisherman, packet rat, smuggler, and man-of-warsman. He's been with me on every ship I've served on from the *Wabash* to the *Monticello*."

Dave poured out coffee for the skipper.

"You seem to take to this life, lad," said Cushing.

"Yes, sir."

"I expected these last two weeks to make you wish you'd swallowed the anchor."

"I'm not a loblolly boy, sir. I served on my father's ship on a voyage to Nassau, and have been up and down the coast from Norfolk to Savannah."

Cushing bowed. "I apologize, Stormalong," he said with an infectious grin.

Dave couldn't help smiling. Will Cushing kept a happy ship. For his years he was more of a man than men twice his age, as Dave had heard more than one of the *Monticello*'s crew say. They took pride in the young man who was known throughout the Navy as one of the most daring men of his time.

"I've made up my mind to sign on, sir," Dave said.

"Enlist, you mean?"

"Yes, sir!"

"You'll have to get your father's permission."

"I don't know where he is."

Cushing eyed David. He had grown to feel a strong attachment for this salty young man he had saved from drowning. There were younger lads than Dave serving in the fleet. "All right!" he said suddenly. "I'll sign you up, and glad to have you!"

"The Captain won't regret it. I know the sounds and rivers, sir."

Cushing studied Dave. "Just what do you mean by that?"

"The whole crew knows the Captain wants to cut out the *Albemarle* if he can get the chance. I know Albemarle Sound, Batchelor's Bay, Roanoke River, and Eastmost River like the palms of my hands by day or night, sir."

Cushing nodded. "I've heard that. But you're too young to poke into places like that. The rebels have ten thousand troops in that area thirsting for fresh Yankee blood. If they should capture you, and you being from that country, it would go hard with you, Davie."

"I'm a Union man, sir!"

Cushing grinned. "How well I know that! Stay below. It's a foul day and my weapons need cleaning. I'll talk to you later."

Dave was left alone in the cabin. He drank some of the coffee and took out the gun-cleaning materials. It was a job he loved, for his father had taught him all about guns and he had often cleaned his father's weapons and used them as well for fowling and hunting. He took Cushing's Sharps carbine from its rack. It had a leather-covered barrel to protect it from salt spray. Cushing had carried it on some of his daring forays into the tidal sounds and rivers of the coast. Dave took out the breechblock and cleaned the inside of the barrel until it glistened. He cleaned the breechblock and rubbed linseed oil into the stock. Then he stripped down the heavy Navy Colt and cleaned it. Last of all he took the ornate dress sword and wiped it carefully.

He shut the door and then buckled the gunbelt about

his slim waist and slid the Colt into its holster. He hung, the sword from its sling and took the carbine in his hands. He could envision himself following Cushing ashore in the dark o' the moon for some daring foray that would make his name as well known as that of Will Cushing.

After a time he took off the belt and hung it up, then replaced the carbine in its rack and the sword on its pegs. He was nothing but a substitute cabin boy. Not for him would be the uniform of a midshipman, a " reefer " with gold anchors on his lapels, a double row of bright brass buttons, a visored cap, and a sword.

Will Cushing was just seven years older than Dave, and he commanded a fine ship like the *Monticello,* but strangely enough, although he had attended the Naval Academy at Annapolis, he had left the Academy before his graduation, later being appointed an acting master's mate in the United States Volunteer Navy. He had served on various ships of the Home and Blockading Squadron, seeing some action, and had been appointed a midshipman. Cushing had served aboard the *Cambridge* when the *Merrimac* had attacked Union vessels at Hampton Roads and had been slightly wounded by one of her shells. In 1862 he had been appointed lieutenant and had requested duty with his friend and hero, Lieutenant Commander Flusser, the " fighting man of the North Carolina sounds." He had seen a great deal of hot action with Flusser and had later been given command of his own vessel at the age of nineteen years.

Dave had learned a great deal about Cushing during his weeks aboard the *Monticello:* that he had fought infantry close in shore with his ship; that, although he had never been known to take his own safety into account, he was extremely solicitous of his ships and his crews; that he was a strict disciplinarian and a first-rate seaman with the most loyal crews in the Navy.

Cushing had raided Confederate installations ashore, barely avoiding capture more than once, and was always in the thick of the fight. He had volunteered more than once to serve ashore as a battery commander in the Army.

Cushing had taken command of the fine and fast *Monticello* for distinguished services rendered and had taken her from Philadelphia to duty off the North Carolina coast as part of the North Atlantic Blockading Squadron, which had as its beat the coast line from Chesapeake Bay to Cape Fear.

The door of the cabin was slid open, and Will Cushing came in with dripping oilskins. " We're in for a blow, boy," he said. He eyed his weapons. " You do a good job, Davie."

" Thank you, sir."

The officer hung up his oilskins. " I'm getting bored with offshore blockading duty," he said.

" It might win the war, sir."

" Yes, but it's a rough duty. Do you realize that the entire blockade stretches for thirty-five hundred miles, from Alexandria on the Potomac, along the sweep of the Atlantic Coast to the Florida Capes, then across the Gulf of Mexico to the mouth of the Rio Grande? "

" That's a lot of salt water," said Dave dryly.

" I saw a report on blockading duty when I was in Washington last year. We of the Navy have to patrol a maze of one hundred and eighty-nine bays, inlets, and harbors. Right now we have thirty vessels off Cape Fear alone. The ships of deep draft usually anchor at night to keep in formation with a lee shore astern, shoals, contrary currents, easterly winds always blowing, with a rough cross chop set up when the ebb tide is met. Ground tackle is strained and cables snap; anchors drag and ships go aground."

" But it is successful, isn't it, sir? "

Cushing smiled. " Yes. I think we average capturing or driving ashore about seventy-five per cent of the blockade-runners."

" But what about the *Albemarle*, Captain? "

There was a worried look on the officer's long, bony face. " The Navy has strengthened the blockading squadron off Plymouth. Torpedoes as well as obstructions have been placed at the mouth of the Roanoke River. But, as yet, we have no vessel capable of beating her in Albemarle Sound."

Every member of the *Monticello*'s crew knew the obsession Cushing had of getting a chance to attack the huge ram, and they all knew he would attack it bare-handed if he had the chance.

～

It was dusk when a lookout spied the dim topsails of a ship. Dave stood at the rail with Scrimshaw. " A blockade-runner or commerce destroyer? " asked Dave.

" No. She's one of ours. The *Rhode Island*, I think. See! There goes her kerosene signal lantern."

Many of the crew lined the rails. They were always eager for news, as blockading duty, despite its moments of excitement, could also be mighty boring and monotonous. Virile men, such as composed the crew of the *Monticello*, could while away only so much of their time with fancy ropework, making ships in bottles, and doing scrimshaw work, which was fancy-carved work in bone or wood, from which Scrimshaw Appleby had earned his nickname. His sea chest was full of carved fans, nutcrackers, heads of men, and animals and little ships.

The signal lamp blinked out on the other ship, and a moment later the signalman on the quarter-deck of the *Monticello* began to signal a reply. Clack-click-click it went on until the reply was finished, and then there was an answer from the other ship. Then both ships sailed on through the darkness.

In a short time the crew knew what had been sent from the other ship, the *Rhode Island:* the *Monticello* was to sail to Beaufort for further orders.

" Suits me," said Taffy Brown. " I've had enough of moldy sea biscuits, foul coffee, damp berth decks, and no chance of shore leave. When the war is over, I'll place an oar on me shoulder and walk inland until some rube asks me what it is I have on me shoulder, and it is there I will settle down."

Scrimshaw spat to leeward. " Ye'll never cut your painter loose from the Navy, Taffy."

Dave looked toward the west. The coast was out of sight and had been for days, but he was eager to get ashore to see if he could find news about his father. If Micah Scott had reached Halifax safely, he would surely return south to learn what had happened to David.

Scrimshaw placed a hand on Dave's shoulder. " Belike ye'll hear news of your father," he said. It was almost as if he had read Dave's mind.

" I know he'll join the Navy again if they'll take him, with one arm and all."

" Aye, lad! From what ye've told me about him he is as good a man with one arm as any man with two arms."

The course of the ship was changed, and the trim *Monticello* began to beat against a strong wind as she started for Cape Lookout and Bogue Sound.

Chapter 6

THE U.S.S. *Monticello* lay at anchor off Beaufort. At one time, before the war, the sleepy town had been known for its fishing and cotton-shipping business, but now the streets were filled with Union soldiers and sailors. Supplies for the blockading squadron were piled high on the wharves, and Union vessels were moored to them or lay in the stream at anchor. There was a curious assembly of vessels there, and many of them had never been intended for naval use.

There were broad-beamed ferryboats carrying heavy guns. There were commercial steamers and sailing vessels that had been taken into the Navy. A tugboat from New York was set up on ways at a small shipyard for work to be done on her hull, which had taken a terrible pounding on the trip down from the north. There were swift double-ended side-wheelers of shallow draft, ideal for use in the tidal rivers, for they could go forward or backward with equal ease instead of being forced to turn around in the narrow channels.

Beaufort had been occupied by Union troops for about two years after the capture of New Berne on the Neuse

River. David had been there many times on his father's vessel, the *Alice*, and he was eager to get ashore.

Cushing came down from the quarter-deck of the *Monticello*. His gig lay at the side of the ship. He looked at David. " Come ashore with me, David. We'll try to get news of your father."

" Can I enlist here, sir? "

Cushing nodded. " You're sure you want to? "

" Yes, sir! "

Cushing shrugged. They got into the gig and were pulled ashore, with Scrimshaw handling the tiller. Lieutenant Cushing got out of the boat and waited on the wharf for David and Scrimshaw. " You're fifteen now, are you not, David? " asked the officer.

" Yes, sir, just this past week."

Cushing nodded. " You'll be in the Navy within a few hours then."

~

It was late afternoon when David walked back toward the wharves with Scrimshaw. He had been examined physically and then sworn into the United States Volunteer Navy, with Will Cushing signing his papers for him. Now he could return aboard the *Monticello* as a full-fledged member of her crew. He looked out at the fine ship. The only thing that spoiled his excitement was the fact that he had not been able to get any news of his father.

They pulled out to the *Monticello* and went aboard. Lieutenant Cushing had stayed in town, and all the officers were ashore too, leaving a master's mate in charge of the ship.

Cushing had been free with shore leave, and there was only a skeleton crew aboard the vessel. David reported in to draw his issue of uniforms and equipment, and later he carried it down to the berth deck to mark his clothing with his name.

The berth deck was empty except for Steve Raintree, another boy, who had been the pet of the crew until David had come along. Steve had a shock of straw-colored hair and a face that seemed to be entirely composed of freckles and from which peered two intensely blue eyes. Steve was a veteran. He had been aboard the U.S.S. *Ellis* with Will Cushing when Cushing had gone up the New River to Jacksonville, the county seat of Onslow County, and raided it. They had captured two small schooners and raised the Stars and Stripes over the courthouse.

The *Ellis* had not been able to get back over the bar, and they had stayed there watching rebel watch fires along the shore. Two artillery pieces had opened up on the *Ellis*, but they had managed to drive the rebels from their position by accurate shooting with their forward eighty-pounder rifle. Later the *Ellis* had gone aground, and in the ensuing action when the *Ellis* had been shelled by rebel shore batteries, Steve had been wounded in the shoulder, but he had stayed on at his post of duty. Later they had been forced to abandon the *Ellis* and had escaped in one of the small schooners they had captured. Since that time Steve Raintree had served with Cushing.

Dave ignored the tough young veteran. He was a little older than David and a little heavier, and more than once he had hazed Dave as a greenhorn. Dave was marking his clothing when he heard the slap of bare feet behind him. Suddenly a foot capsized his ink bottle, and the black ink spread across the deck and soaked swiftly into the holystoned wood. Dave was aghast. It would be up to him to clean it up before the bosun saw the stain. He looked up at Steve.

Steve grinned. " Sloppy landsman," he said.

" I'm no landsman," said David. " I've just enlisted."

" We must be losing the war then. Enlisting greenhorns and rebels to boot."

Dave stood up. " I've told you more than once that I'm no rebel, Raintree."

The boy raised his head. " Try and stop me," he said.

" I don't want to fight."

" I figured you wouldn't."

" If Jimmylegs catches us, we'll have to go before the mast."

" He ain't aboard, sonny."

They stood there watching each other. Then Steve placed a bare foot on the spilled ink and began to spread it around as much as possible.

It was too much for David. He shoved the boy back against the side of the ship. Raintree grinned again. Suddenly his right first shot out, catching Dave on the jaw and dumping him neatly right on top of the wet ink. Dave got up slowly. Steve had a wallop like a kicking mule. Before Steve could get his hands up, Dave was upon him, battering away with both fists.

Steve was stronger than David, but Dave had the speed on him. Dave circled, throwing punches from all angles, hitting Steve twice for every blow he took in return. They separated. Blood flowed from Steve's nose, but he was still full of fight. He rushed David and drove him full across the deck to the portside of the ship near a square opening that let in the wind and sun. Dave went down, hitting

59

his head against the side of the ship. He slid down onto the deck.

Steve danced about, throwing punches and looking fierce with blood running from his smashed nose. " Get up, *rebel*," he cried. " I ain't through whipping you yet! "

Dave felt his jaw. " You haven't whipped anybody yet," he said quietly. He stood up and raised his fists.

Steve launched a ferocious attack, and Dave was hit three times before he got the range and shook the boy with a hard right hook. Steve jumped back, shook his head, and then rushed David, with his head down and both fists battering away. Dave hit him once on the side of the head and then stepped aside to avoid being driven helplessly against the side of the ship. Steve plowed on, right through the opening, and yelled in horror as he felt nothing but air beneath his churning feet. He struck the water with a tremendous splash.

Dave couldn't help laughing, battered as he was. He looked down at the water. Steve came up, gulping air. " I can't swim too good! " he yelled, and then he went under again.

Dave peeled off blouse and trousers, poised himself, and then dove cleanly into the water. He went down deep and saw a dim, struggling figure close to him. He reached out and gripped Steve by his shock of yellow hair. He swam upward with one arm and broke the surface, pulling Steve's head out of the water. " Don't struggle," he warned.

A heaving line shot down from the deck, and Dave gripped it. He saw a boat pulling toward them, and in the stern was Jimmylegs, the tough master-at-arms. They were pulled into the boat and climbed dripping to the deck.

" What is this? " roared Jimmylegs.

The two boys looked at each other.

" Get below, you lubbers! "

They went down the ladder to the berth deck, followed by Jimmylegs. He placed his big fists on his hips and bent head forward. " Well? " he demanded. " Who spilled that ink? "

" I did," said Dave quietly.

" Then what happened? "

Steve raised his head. " I . . ."

Dave stepped forward. " I spilled the ink. Raintree got excited and fell overboard. I went in after him. That's all, master-at-arms."

Jimmylegs looked from one to the other of them. " So? That's the truth, Raintree? "

" I . . ."

Dave spoke up again. " It's the truth, sir."

" Fine pair of lubbers! What's the Navy coming to? Spilling ink on the deck! Falling overboard! I should have you up before the mast for this! "

Scrimshaw came down the ladder. " I'll help them clean it up, Jimmylegs."

The master-at-arms nodded. " I want that deck spotless before mess! " he bellowed; then he left the berth deck.

Scrimshaw eyed the two dripping boys. " What happened to your nose, Steve? " he asked.

" Fell up a mast, Scrimshaw," said Steve.

Scrimshaw nodded. " I'll get some cleaning materials." He went aft along the berth deck.

Steve looked ashamed as he eyed Dave. " I'm sorry," he said. He fingered his nose. " You carry a wallop like a hundred-pound columbiad," he said.

61

Dave grinned. He thrust out a hand. " Shipmates? " he asked.

Steve smiled and held out his hand. " *Shipmates!* "

~

In the days that followed Dave's fight with Steve, he was kept too busy to think very much. The rigging of the ship had to be set up tighter. Sails were taken down and mended. He learned the use of sailor's palm and needle under the skilled tutelage of Sails, the sailmaker, who was responsible for much of the training of boys and green hands.

Working on the intricate rigging was quite a chore. Dave learned the uses of fids, serving mallets, toggles, prickers, marlinespikes, palms, and heavers. His hands toughened with the work. Betweentimes, he learned how to serve the guns and keep them bright and clean. He pulled an oar in the big cutter and also spent some of his free time teaching his new shipmate Steve how to swim better.

The days went by swiftly, and one day Steve and Dave took out the small gig under sail to look at some of the other ships moored off Beaufort.

" There's a double-ender I ain't seen around here," said Steve as he came about and bent his head under the shifting sail.

Dave looked at the vessel that was churning toward them. She was a fast side-wheel steamer, with one tall funnel and two masts, schooner-rigged, and her sharp prow had been fitted with a heavy-looking bronze beak for ramming.

" I see her name," said Steve as he eased the sheet. " The

Sassacus. I've heard it said she's the fastest double-ender in the fleet."

The *Sassacus* slowed down, and then her paddle wheels went into reverse to help slow her way. She coasted easily toward shore, and then her anchor went down and she swung with the current.

The boys sailed closer to her. " She carries four Dahlgren guns for broadsides and two Parrott rifles," said Dave.

Steve grinned. " My, my, but you sure are the gunner's mate, though."

" What's the news, matey? " yelled Dave to a seaman who stood on the deck of the *Sassacus.*

" Trouble on Albemarle Sound," said the seaman. " The *Albemarle* came down the Roanoke to Plymouth and passed the obstructions. Our shore guns had little effect on her. She met the *Southfield* and the *Miami* in the river."

" What happened then? " asked Steve.

" Our two vessels were lashed together, the idea of Commander Flusser, of the *Miami,* so that he could get the ram in between his two vessels so as to have her at a disadvantage. But the ram eluded them and rammed the *Southfield* and sank her.

" Commander Flusser pulled the lanyard of one of his forward guns, but the nine-inch shot merely bounced back from the plating of the ram and killed him. The crew of the *Miami* tried to board the *Albemarle* but were driven off, and the *Miami* retreated."

Dave looked at Steve. " Flusser dead. What will Captain Cushing think? Flusser was his shipmate and hero."

The seaman spat into the water. " When the fight was over, the rebel general Hoke attacked Plymouth, and with the help of the ram, he captured the town along with six-

63

teen hundred Union men and twenty-five pieces of artillery. The *Albemarle* is queen of the sound now. We have nothing to stop her."

A man came aft to where the seaman was standing. He had only one arm, the right one, and Dave's heart leaped within him. "Father!" he yelled in delight.

Micah Scott rushed to the rail and thrust down his arm. Dave gripped it and was pulled easily up onto the deck. Micah Scott had tears in his eyes as he bearhugged David with his arm. "I never thought I'd see you again," he said softly.

"What are you doing here?"

"I'm master's mate on the *Sassacus*, newly assigned. I got to Halifax, then took ship for New York, and the train to Washington. I was appointed master's mate, and I requested duty in this squadron. They sent me to the *Sassacus* and here I am."

They went to the galley to get coffee, trailed by Steve. Dave told his father everything that had happened, but he hesitated to tell him he had enlisted.

Micah Scott tugged at his beard. "I'll send you up north to Baltimore," he said. "Your aunt will take you in and send you to school."

Steve grinned. "After he gets his discharge," he said.

Micah Scott stared at Dave. "You enlisted?"

"Yes, sir."

"A child like you?"

Steve grinned. "Some baby," he said.

Dave looked up at his father. "How old were you when you went to sea aboard the old *Constellation*?"

"What has that to do with you?"

"How old?" persisted Dave.

" Sixteen! "

Dave shook his head. " You were thirteen, Dad, and you know it."

Micah Scott looked away. " All right . . . all right. I knew you'd enlist someday."

" I'm on a good ship, sir. The *Monticello*. Lieutenant Cushing commands her."

" That wild daredevil? He'll get all of you into trouble from what I've heard about him."

Steve touched his left shoulder. " Yeh," he said dryly.

Micah Scott stood up. " I'll have you transferred aboard the *Sassacus*," he said.

Dave opened his mouth and then shut it. He didn't want to leave the *Monticello,* and his good shipmates Scrimshaw, Steve, Taffy Brown, Frank Richmond, Ginger, and above all, Will Cushing, but he knew his father would have his way.

" Got to keep an eye on you," said Micah.

" Yes, sir."

" Get back aboard your ship. I'll be over to see Mister Cushing later today."

They cast off from the *Sassacus,* and not a word passed between them as they tacked toward their ship. They made the gig fast to the *Monticello* and clambered aboard. Steve looked at Dave. " I'm happy for you, shipmate," he said, " but I hate to see you leave the *Monticello.* This old tub won't be quite the same no more."

Chapter 7

THE *Sassacus* tugged gently at its anchor with the flow of the tide in Albermarle Sound. Seven Union vessels in all were anchored in the sound. In addition to the *Sassacus* there were three other double-enders, the *Mattabesett*, the *Wyalusing*, and the *Miami*. There was the *Commodore Hull*, a converted ferryboat with heavy armament, and two gunboats, the *Whitehead* and the *Ceres*. All of them formed the little squadron of tough old Captain Melancton Smith, who had been sent to the sound by Admiral Lee to stop, as best he could, the threat of the formidable *Albemarle* should she venture down the sound.

Dave Scott vigorously polished one of the four nine-inch Dahlgren guns of the *Sassacus*. He had been kept busy enough on the double-ender since he had left the *Monticello*. The *Sassacus* was commanded by Lieutenant Commander Francis A. Roe, and that bearded officer and gentleman kept a taut and happy ship.

The squadron lay off Bluff Point almost midway in the stream between the low shores. The May sun was bright and cheerful. The sun glistened from polished gun barrels and the brass fittings of some of the vessels. An officers' meeting had been called, and the commanders and officers of the squadron were all aboard the *Mattabesett*. Their gigs were moored alongside the double-ender, and every seaman and gunner in the unit kept an eye on her. Rumors were rife aboard every one of the vessels. Something was in the wind.

Assistant-Surgeon Holden stopped beside David. " You'll wear that gun barrel clean through, Davie," he said.

Dave stepped back and looked at his handiwork. " Sponge me dry and keep me clean, and I'll fire a shot to Calais Green," he said, patting the thick barrel of the Dahlgren.

Holden grinned. " We may have to use all our guns before too long," he said.

" Sir, do you think we'll go in after the *Albermarle*? "

" More likely *she'll* come out after *us*," said the surgeon dryly.

" One against seven? "

" Yes, one ironclad, with heavy Brooke rifles and a massive ram against wooden ships."

Gigs were pulling away from the *Mattabesett*. The sun glistened from the wet oars as they dipped and rose steadily.

Holden filled and lighted his meerschaum pipe. " My nose for battle tells me we won't have long to wait to sniff gunpowder."

Dave nodded. The crew of the *Sassacus* were acting busy at their various chores, but their eyes were on the gig carrying the officers of their vessel. Just the week before, on April 29, the *Albemarle* had brought back a steamer that the Confederates had captured on the Alligator River. On her trip to pick up the steamer she had chased off a

Union gunboat. The whole affair had stung the Union squadron which had controlled those waters for so long.

The *Albemarle* had picked up the steamer and some corn barges and had returned triumphantly back to Plymouth, while the Union vessels had stayed miles away near Roanoke Island, unable to do a thing to stop her. She was queen of the sound now, and there wasn't a Union vessel capable of stopping her.

Things had been going from bad to worse for the Navy. They had lost their coal at Plymouth and had requested coal from General Ben Butler, the politician turned soldier. Butler had outlined a plan whereby several small Army gunboats would "run down" the *Albemarle*, but there had been a bitter controversy over whether the Army or the Navy should have jurisdiction over the gunboats. Butler, in a fit of pique, had refused to give the Navy enough coal to keep steam up, and when they had protested, he had told them to go to captured Plymouth and get their coal stores back from the rebels.

Butler had stoked the fire of controversy by blaming the Navy for the loss of Plymouth. Butler had ideas of replacing Abraham Lincoln as the Republican candidate for the fall presidential election and would do anything to build up his reputation.

The gig pulled alongside, and the captain got up onto the deck of the *Sassacus*. "Mister Mayer," he said to the young ensign, "have the crew fall into quarters. I wish to address them."

The bosun's pipe shrilled at a command from Mayer, and the crew fell into line. Dave stood in the rear rank. His father stood between Acting Master Boutelle and Chief Engineer Hobby.

68

Captain Roe folded his arms across his chest. "Men," he said, "we have news that the *Albemarle* may soon come down from Plymouth. The duty of this squadron is to stop her. Our plan of attack is for the larger vessels to pass as close as possible to the ram without endangering their paddle wheels, deliver their fire, and then round to for a second discharge.

"The smaller vessels are to take care of some thirty armed launches that are expected to accompany the ram. The *Miami* will carry a torpedo to be exploded under the *Albermarle*, and a strong net, or seine, to foul her propeller.

"You gun captains must watch your chance to get a shot into her ports when they are open. It will take timing and skill, but you can do it.

"We must be careful to avoid being run down as the *Southfield* was. The fore- and after-pivot Parrott rifles must aim for the roof, ports, hull, and smokestack to seek a weak spot.

"We will go into action with each man armed with cutlass and boarding pistols in case we get a chance to close with her. We have a three-ton bronze beak on our prow and the swiftest ship in the squadron, and it is my intention to close with her and sink her."

The crew broke into spontaneous cheers. Dave warmed to them. He had never forgotten his shipmates on the *Monticello*, but now the crew of the saucy *Sassacus* rated just as high with him.

Roe held up his hand. "The plan of battle is for the squadron to advance in two lines. The first line will be led by the *Mattabesett*, followed by the *Sassacus*, *Wyalusing*, and *Whitehead*. The second line will be led by the *Miami*, followed by the *Ceres* and the *Commodore Hull*. All vessels will carry nets and lines and will to try foul the *Albemarle's* propeller, but the *Miami* is to have first chance at her with her net. Ramming is optional . . ." Here the officer smiled, and every man on deck knew what he was thinking about; the *Sassacus would* ram, and be the first to do so if at all possible.

The crew was dismissed. Acting Master's Mate Micah Scott beckoned to his son and then walked aft with him. "This will be a dangerous action, Davie. I know better than to try to get you off this vessel. Younger boys than you have fought and died on the decks of the ships of the United States Navy. What is your post?"

"Powder monkey on the forward pivot gun sir."

Micah Scott paled a little. "Well, it can't be helped."

It was time for noon mess, and they parted. Dave ate with his messmates, and there was very little talk among them. Dave had once heard about the patriotic speeches men made to one another on the eve of action, but he heard none of them in the messroom of the *Sassacus*. The only thing he noted was the lack of appetites among his messmates.

~

By the middle of the afternoon the *Sassacus* was ready for action. The awnings had been housed and the decks cleared of anything that might splinter and kill or wound men. Boarding nets had been rigged along the rails, leaving gaps where the guns poked their black muzzles over the sides. Shell, solid shot, and canister were placed near the guns. A gunner's mate was busy placing grenades where they would be handy in case of a close-in action.

Dave walked aft and looked at the six other vessels of

70

the squadron. They were all ready. Wisps of steam drifted from their tall smokestacks as engineers got up steam. It was May 5, 1864, and 3:30 in the afternoon.

Dave thought of the many times he had plied those waters in the little and dainty *Alice.* He had poked into many of the sound inlets in his little skiff and knew them well, but he had never imagined in his wildest dreams that he would be serving aboard a Union warship in those waters, waiting for one of the most formidable armored vessels in the world to poke her nose down the sound.

He leaned against the jack staff and thought back on the *Albemarle,* with her solid pine framing and sheathing plated with four inches of iron; of the two powerful Brooke rifles with their hundred-pound projectiles; of the solid wooden ram plated with two-inch iron; and of the two powerful engines that would drive the ram toward her wooden-hulled opponents. " Like a hot knife through butter," he said aloud.

" You talking to me, boy? " asked the gun captain of the port after nine-inch Dahlgren gun.

" No."

The gunner patted the breech of his charge. " Let me at that blasted rebel iron pot," he said.

" She might not come after all."

The gunner looked up the sound. " No? " he said quietly. " Look."

A streamer of smoke was rising to the west, and two other smaller streamers showed behind it.

" Beat to quarters! " called out Lieutenant Commander Roe from the foredeck.

The young drummer of the *Sassacus* ran to the quarterdeck and raised his sticks. Then he began to beat the

71

long roll, steadily and loudly. In a moment the drums aboard the other vessels began to thud and rumble.

Coal scoops rattled in the fireroom of the double-ender. Thick black smoke began to rise from the smokestacks of the Union squadron. A signalman aboard the *Mattabesett* began to wave his flags.

The crew of the *Sassacus* took their stations. The anchor was broken free from the bottom, hauled up, and catted. The paddle wheels began to turn slowly, holding the craft against the strong current.

The *Mattabesett* began to forge ahead, followed by the *Sassacus* and the others. They began to move toward Sandy Point.

" Cast loose and provide! " came the command.

The gun crews prepared their charges for action. Powder bags were rammed into the gaping muzzles followed by the projectiles. Riflemen climbed up into the rigging, carrying bags of grenades.

Dave was at his position near the forward Parrott rifle under the command of Ensign Mayer. He wet his dry lips and fought down a queasiness in his belly. He glanced back to where his father was stationed near the wheel. Micah Scott knew those waters like the palm of his right hand.

" There they are! " said Ensign Mayer.

The ram looked like a huge, slab-sided turtle, and there wasn't a sign of life aboard her. Black smoke gushed from her stack, and the Confederate flag snapped in the breeze, half obscured by the billowing smoke. Behind the ram were two other vessels, one of them much smaller than the other.

" The big steamer is the *Cotton Plant*," said a gunner.

" I think the little one is the *Bombshell*," said Dave.

Lieutenant Commander Roe raised his field glasses. " The *Cotton Plant* is loaded with troops," he said quietly.

The *Mattabesett* edged toward the southern side of the sound. The line followed her, with the frash-frash-frash of the paddle wheels and the puffing of the steam exhausts getting louder and louder as they gained speed. The water was calm, with hardly a ripple, and the prows of the vessels going into the attack cut cleanly through it, casting long foamy wakes behind them, while the *Albemarle*, with its broad heavy hull, seemed to be piling water up ahead of it as it pushed on.

The gunners of the *Sassacus* stared at the immense ram. Loaders, shotmen, tacklemen, and trainers were ready. " Look alive! " roared Ensign Mayer. The ram's forward gun-port stopper had dropped to the deck, and the snout of a Brooke rifle appeared. The puff of smoke showed almost as though by magic, followed by the heavy thud of the gun. The shell smashed close to the pivot rifle of the *Mattabesett*, cutting away rails and spars. Men dropped to the deck as though flung there by an unseen giant hand.

The ram forged on toward the *Mattabesett*, firing steadily. The double-ender skillfully eluded her while opening fire with her guns. The shock and roar of the discharges echoed across the water.

The *Sassacus* was next in line. A broadside from the nine-inch guns blasted out, and the projectiles clanged against the iron carapace of the *Albemarle* and bounded harmlessly into the air.

" Pivot gun, fire! " commanded Ensign Mayer.

The gun captain jerked the lanyard, and the Parrott roared defiance. Stinking smoke blew back over the gun crew, and the one-hundred-pound solid shot bounced from the sloping roof of the *Albemarle.*

" Run in! " yelled the gun captains of the broadside guns.

Tacklemen sprang into action and heaved until the guns ran back. Sponge-rammers plunged into the smoking throats of the Dahlgrens and pulled clear. Powder bags went in, followed by the projectiles.

" Stand clear! " the gun captains commanded. " Run out! Fire! "

The Dahlgrens spat flame and smoke and then reared back in recoil against their hurters. The veteran crews had no time to look at the monster they were fighting. They were regulars, skilled and disciplined. It was load and fire, run in, reload, run out, and fire again in a hades of foul smoke, roaring guns, and the splintering smash of shells.

Dave darted forward with a powder bag as the pivot rifle blasted off. Again the projectile bounced from the *Albemarle* like a rubber ball. It was uncanny; the hulk of the ram, with not a man in sight, fired steadily from her ports, like a great mechanical monster, while the steady gun crews of the *Sassacus* stood on the open deck with nothing between them and hundred-pound shot but their sweat-glistening skins.

Now the whole Union squadron was engaged at close quarters, with the swift double-enders racing in and then sheering off after firing to avoid hitting one of their mates.

The *Albermarle* plowed astern of the *Sassacus.* The *Sassacus* heeled well over as her helm was swung hard aport. The little *Bombshell* appeared through the drifting smoke, and the *Sassacus* took her under fire, hulling her many times.

The after-pivot rifle of the *Sassacus* had not fired as yet.

The raging gun captain swung up onto the rail and flourished his pistol. "Haul down your flag and surrender, or we'll blow you out of the water!" he roared.

The rebel flag came down swiftly.

"Drop out of action and anchor, *Bombshell!*" ordered Lieutenant Commander Roe.

The *Bombshell* drifted astern until she was clear of the battle, and her anchor plunged down into the water.

The *Sassacus* was about four hundred yards from the ram. The *Albemarle* had evaded the *Mattabesett* and now lay broadside to the *Sassacus*.

Lieutenant Commander Roe saw his chance. He turned to Acting Master Boutelle. "Lay her course for the junction of the casemate and the hull!"

Four bells rang out in the engine room. The *Sassacus* charged forward, with a plume of thick black smoke streaming from her smokestack. No guns were fired. All eyes were on the ram.

The gap closed, with water purling back from the ram prow of the *Sassacus*. "All hands, lie down!" commanded Roe.

Dave hit the deck, gripping a powder bag. He could see the huge carapace of the ram through an opening in the railing. He wanted to look away, but the sight fascinated him.

Then the *Albemarle* was within a few feet of the racing *Sassacus*. The double-ender struck with a crash that shook her hull like an earthquake. The *Sassacus* careened, and Dave slid down to the port rail and nearly overside, but a brawny gunner gripped him by the arm and pulled him back. "No time for a swim, messmate," he said with a grin.

The *Sassacus* quivered from stem to stern. The swift plashing of the paddles showed that the engines were unharmed. Dave peered at the ram. A port stopper dropped, and a gun was run out. He could see the gun crew inside. The gun blasted off, and the shell crashed through the flimsy hull of the *Sassacus*. Splinters flew like knives through the smoky air.

The ram moved ahead, twisting the shattered prow of the double-ender. One of the ram's guns was run out and discharged ten feet from the side of the crippled *Sassacus*. There was a shattering roar from below, and steam and hot water gushed up on the canted deck of the *Sassacus*. The overcharged boilers released their contents with banshee screeching that drowned out the roaring of the *Sassacus'* well-served guns.

Rifles rattled from the shrouds of the double-ender. Grenades dropped on the top deck of the ram and exploded as harmlessly as so many firecrackers. The *Sassacus* surged heavily to port.

" She's sinking! " a gunner yelled.

Roe cupped his hands about his mouth. " All hands, repel boarders on starboard bow! "

Dave jumped to his feet and jerked his heavy cutlass from its scabbard. Men rushed up from below, armed with cutlasses and pistols. Some of them had been seared by the escaping steam, but they were ready for further battle.

The *Sassacus'* guns flared through the clinging smoke and steam, hammering away at the iron monster. Projectiles bounded up into the air and splashed into the water.

Dave looked back over his shoulder. There was no sign of boarders, and to send men atop the grated deck of the ram would have been madness. He saw the other ships

76

of the squadron in the distance, lying still in the water while the fighting *Sassacus* carried on the unequal battle alone.

The *Miami* closed in but was yawing and veering badly. The *Wyalusing* was signaling that she was sinking.

"Powder!" screamed Ensign Mayer at Dave.

He snatched up a powder bag and thrust it into the hot muzzle of the big pivot rifle. The ram fired, and the blasting hurled the gun captain and Ensign Mayer to the deck.

The Parrott was depressed and aimed right at the hull of the *Albemarle*. Dave snatched the lanyard from the deck and jerked it. The gun leaped back, and the deck was covered with smoke. "Run in!" yelled Dave. "Load!"

Mayer stood up, holding his head. The gun captain lay unconscious.

"Run out!" commanded Dave. "Stand clear!" He jerked the lanyard again. The projectile smashed against the hull of the ram and shattered. Shards of metal flew back onto the deck of the *Sassacus*, and one of them cut across Dave's left thigh. He felt something warm run down his leg.

Ensign Mayer thrust Dave aside. "Good work, boy! I'll take over! *Powder!*"

A seaman carried the signal books to the rail to hurl them overboard. The *Sassacus* would go down; she *had* to go down. Then she drifted astern of the ram, firing incessantly and taking heavy blows in return from the after port of the *Albemarle*.

The other ships opened fire again. The Confederate colors were shot away. "She's struck!" cried Dave.

But the *Albemarle* was still full of fight, and she kept giving back as much as she took. The fire of the Union vessels became more dangerous to each other than to the ram.

The *Albemarle* was moving slowly away. Her smoke-stack was riddled with shot. The *Miami* shot in to explode her torpedo to no avail. She threw over her net, but it did no good. Then slowly and stubbornly the ram moved up the sound, followed by the Union vessels pouring shot and shell at her. Thick smoke billowed from her riddled smoke-stack. Dusk was falling over the sound as she fled toward Plymouth.

Dave dropped to the deck and ripped back his trouser leg. The thigh was gashed and bleeding profusely, but it wasn't a serious wound.

A seaman came forward. " Davie," he said, " your father wants to see you."

Dave looked up quickly. " Why? "

" He's been wounded."

Then Dave heard the groaning and screaming of wounded and scalded men, and more fear than he had experienced in the battle came over him. The decks were littered with splinters and chunks of wood and metal. The bronze beak at the prow was twisted and almost torn away. Powder-blackened men dropped wearily beside their guns. The smoke drifted off with the wind. But the *Sassacus* was still afloat, though badly damaged. It would be a long time before she was fit for duty again.

Dave hobbled aft. Ensign Mayer gave him a hand. " Boy," he said, " I'll see to it that you get something for your handling of the gun when I was knocked down."

Dave did not answer. His father had suffered enough from the war; it was more than cruel that he should be hurt once more.

78

Chapter 8

THE JULY heat beat down on the wide, dusty streets of Washington. A battery of horse artillery trotted down Pennsylvania Avenue. One of the gunners glanced at Midshipman David Scott as he waited to cross the street. "Hey, sonny!" he yelled. "Ain't you pretty far from salt water?"

"About as far from salt water as you are from the Army of Northern Virginia!" Dave replied.

"A good answer," a quiet voice said behind Dave.

Dave whirled and looked into the smiling face of Will Cushing. "Sir! What are you doing here in Washington?"

Cushing winked. "I'll tell you in private while we have lunch together." He eyed Dave. "A real 'reefer' now? Midshipman Scott, no less. I heard about your part aboard the *Sassacus*. Admiral Lee promoted you for distinguished services rendered, I hear."

Dave flushed. "Every man aboard the *Sassacus* did distinguished service, sir."

Cushing nodded. "How is your father?"

"Not too well. He was struck through the right shoulder by a splinter, and the muscles were damaged. It would

79

have been bad enough for a man with two arms to have been hit so, but he could not use his right arm at all for a time."

"And you, Dave?"

"I was slightly wounded and was sent with my father to the Naval Hospital here. When he was convalescing I was ordered to duty at the Navy Department." Dave shook his head. "Im still there, running errands, filling out forms, filing papers, and doing other chores that just make me sick."

"Is your father here now?"

"No, he is with his sister in Baltimore."

"I see. Let's go to Willard's Hotel, and I'll tell you why I'm here."

They walked toward the hotel and Dave looked up at his hero. "How's Scrimshaw, and Steve Raintree, and Ginger? What about Ensign Howorth? How's the old *Monticello*? Did you run down any more blockade-runners?"

Cushing laughed and held up a hand. "One at a time. One at a time."

～

Will Cushing shoved back the dishes to clear a space on the tablecloth. He took out a pencil and began to sketch Albemarle Sound and the mouth of the Roanoke River. "Your old friend, the *Albemarle*, is moored at Plymouth, which, as you well know, is eight miles up the Roanoke from the sound. A mile below the ram is the wreck of the *Southfield*, with the hurricane deck still above water and with a guard of rebel soldiers aboard it."

Cushing was sketching in details as he talked. "We still do not have an ironclad with shallow enough draft to be able to cross Hatteras Bar and enter the sound to go in after her. Admiral Lee will risk no more wooden vessels, such as your *Sassacus,* to fight her again. It took us a month of spy work to locate exactly where the ram is moored.

" It was decided there was but one way to go in and get her, and that is, with a small-boat raid to cut her out and capture her or blow her up."

Dave leaned forward. It had always been Cushing's one desire to get at the ram that had killed his friend and hero, Flusser.

" Commander Steve Rowan was asked to undertake the expedition, but he refused, saying he did not think the command was practical. Secretary of the Navy Gideon Welles and Gustavus Fox, Assistant Secretary of the Navy, went down a list of possible commanders for the expedition without picking out a man. Admiral Lee sent for me and asked me if I'd undertake the task."

" Foolish question," grinned Dave.

" I haven't forgotten Charley Flusser," said Cushing grimly.

The officer leaned forward. " I suggested two plans. One was to approach the *Albemarle* through the swamps with a party of about one hundred men. We would carry an India-rubber boat that might be inflated to torpedo the ram. The second idea was to use two very small low-pressure steamers armed with torpedoes and howitzers. One of them could dash in and attack, covered by howitzer fire from the other, which in turn would go in if the first boat failed."

Dave whistled softly.

Cushing ran his pencil across the white cloth, up the sound to the Roanoke, and thence to the place where he had marked the position of the ram. He stabbed the pencil down so hard that he broke the point. " It can be done! " he said.

" And you're here in Washington for that purpose? "

" Yes! "

" And has the plan been O.K.'d by the Secretary of the Navy? "

Cushing tapped his coat. " I have orders here in my pocket to proceed forthwith to the Brooklyn Navy Yard to purchase suitable vessels for the operation! " Cushing smiled. " Gustavus Fox wasn't too enthusiastic about the operation, but I talked him into it. He thinks he's sending me to my death."

Dave wet his lips. " Sir, I know those waters almost as well as my father does. I'm sick of shore duty, riding convoy on papers and ink bottles. Let me go with you, sir! "

Cushing leaned back in his chair. " You've already seen your share of danger, Davie."

Dave sat up straight. " I'm big enough and old enough to do a man's work. I know small boats and the Albemarle Sound country. Let me go with you, sir, at least back to duty with the North Atlantic Blockading Squadron. You have influence in the Navy Department."

Cushing grinned. He leaned across the table and gripped Dave's shoulder. " All right, Davie! You can go with me to New York as my aide. I can fix it up. We *Monticello* shipmates ought to stick together." He stood up and reached for his officer's cap.

Dave took the stub of pencil and sharpened it. He ran lines through the drawing Cushing had made on the cloth. " Best not to leave this around where anyone might figure out what it is."

Cushing eyed him. He placed his cap on his head. "You know, Davie, I think you're going to be of some use to me on this expedition after all."

Dave wasn't too worried about Will Cushing's being turned down. He had had friends in the Navy Department since before the war, and his splendid record during the war had marked him as a man to be watched. They knew what he was capable of, and they would never have picked him out for the hazardous *Albemarle* expedition if they had not thought he was probably the most suitable choice for it.

—

The Brooklyn Navy Yard was a bedlam of confusion, thought Dave, as he walked through it with Will Cushing. It sent his thoughts back to the December day when he had seen the ram *Albemarle* for the first time. But there was a great deal of difference between the trampled cornfield on the banks of the Roanoke River, where the ram had been built, and the bustling Brooklyn Navy Yard, where things were sparked by Yankee drive and ingenuity.

There were naval vessels of every type at the yard: screw sloops, screw gunboats known as "ninety-day" gunboats because of the rapidity with which they were built, double-enders such as Dave's old ship the *Sassacus*, single-turreted *Monitor*-type vessels, double-turreted monitors of the *Monadnock* type, propellers, side-wheelers, rams, ironclads, tinclads which were so-called because of their thin armor, frigates and ships of the line of the old sailing-ship navy, mortar-vessels, and the usual small craft necessary for the successful operation of a navy. It was these last in which Will Cushing was interested, and armed with his orders from Gustavus Fox, he was allowed to poke into every part of the yard in his quest.

The yard was a place of organized confusion. It was piled high with guns, spars, sails, anchors, blocks and deadeyes, coils of cable and lines of chains. There were sail lofts, carpenter shops, foundries, gun sheds, paint shops, and shops of many other types.

Will Cushing and Dave spent their time amidst the smaller craft. There were gigs, wherries, cutters, whaleboats, launches, and steam launches, and it was the last of these that narrowed down the search, for Cushing had not been able to find suitable rubber boats for his expedition.

A number of open picket boats were being built, and Cushing selected two of them. They were built of wood and had copper-sheathed bottoms, forty-five feet long and nine feet six inches in beam, and drew about three and a half feet of water. They had low-pressure boilers and small but powerful engines turning small propellers.

Dave was kept busy running his legs off on errands for Lieutenant Cushing, and he learned the hard way what was meant by a leg man.

Cushing planned to fit each of the launches with a twelve-pound howitzer to be placed in the bows. The torpedo device that was to be used was the invention of Engineer John L. Lay, of the Navy, and had been introduced by Chief Engineer W. W. Wood. It was a rather complicated device, but it was the only one that could possibly be used, and so Cushing accepted it for his expedition.

Dave accompanied Lieutenant Cushing to a secluded place on the Hudson River. They tested several torpedoes. The device had many defects and had to be kept in perfect condition. It could be exploded well enough if one had the leisure to do it — which would be far from the case in an attack on the *Albermarle*.

Dave had a mechanical turn of mind that he had inherited from his father, and he studied with interest the way the torpedo would be carried by the launches and how the device would be fired.

A boom, or spar, fourteen feet in length, was rigged out on the starboard side of each launch, and attached to the bluff of the bow by a gooseneck hinge. A topping lift was attached to the free end of the boom and thence run up to a stanchion placed in the center of the launch forward of the boiler. There was a block or pulley at the top of the stanchion, and the topping-lift line passed through it to a small windlass situated in the bottom of the boat. By this means the boom could be swung out and raised or lowered as required.

The torpedo itself was attached to the free end of the boom by means of an iron slide or socket. The torpedo could be detached from the slide by means of a lanyard, or heel jigger, which pulled out a pin, allowing the torpedo to float upward from beneath the water, and in the case of the attack on the ram, the idea was to do this under the hull of the vessel.

The torpedo itself was rather complicated. It was pointed conically at the lower end, and more than half the case was filled with powder, with a metal tube running through it, and had an air chamber at the upper end. At the air-chamber end of the torpedo was a grapeshot, held in place in the tube by a pin which could be detached by another line or lanyard once the torpedo was in proper position.

When the grapeshot was released, it dropped down

through the tube to the tip of the torpedo where a percussion cap was placed on a nipple. The weight of the grapeshot exploded the percussion cap which in turn exploded the powder charge.

When the boom was not in use, it could be swung around by means of a stern line and made fast to the side of the launch. To use the apparatus, the torpedo was put in place, the spar was swung forward and lowered under the water to the desired position, and the pin lanyard was pulled to release the torpedo and allow it to float upward; then the device was fired by drawing steadily on the lanyard which held the grapshot pin in place.

Cushing himself planned to position and fire the torpedo, and Dave couldn't help wondering how a man could make all the complicated maneuvers of positioning and firing the device while under cannon and musketry fire and exposed in an open boat. For the first time since he had known Will Cushing he began to have grave misgivings.

~

It was a warm September day as Dave stood on the wharf looking down on the two trim launches, fresh in their new paint, and with their engines and boilers unsullied by use.

"Ahoy, reefer!" a familiar voice called from behind Dave.

Dave whirled. Scrimshaw Appleby was walking in his rolling gait toward Dave, carrying his sea bag over his shoulder. He was girt with a thick leather belt, from which hung cutlass and Navy Colt, and he carried a Sharps carbine in his free hand.

Dave gripped the old sailor so hard he gasped for

breath. " Easy, matey! " he said.

" What are you doing here? "

Scrimshaw looked down at the two launches. " I talked Mister Howorth into letting me come along to take one of these two smokejacks south."

" An old stick-and-string man like you? "

Scrimshaw dropped his sea bag. " I'm stick and string all right, but I ain't *old*, matey! "

" Who else is coming along? "

Scrimshaw scratched in his beard. " Ensign Howorth is in charge of Picket Boat Number One, and Ensign Andy Stockholm of Number Two. I'm to go in Number One, along with Acting Third Assistant Engineer Bill Stotesbury, First Class Fireman Sam Higgins, Landsman Lorenzo Deming, Landsman Hank Wilkes, Landsman Bob King, and Midshipman Davie Scott."

Dave nearly fell into the filthy water. " *Me?* "

" Yep."

" What about Lieutenant Cushing? "

Scrimshaw shook his head.

" You mean he isn't to command the expedition after all? "

" I didn't say that! I just saw him near the gate. Says to tell you he got a leave en route, and is going home to Fredonia for a spell, while we take the boats down to Albemarle Sound. He'll join us at Hampton Roads, I think. Last thing he told me was to take care of you."

" How will we go? "

Scrimshaw sat on a bollard and looked down at the two launches. " Smokejacks! " he said in a sour voice. He spat clear over them. " We take the canal route to Chesapeake Bay. First we go through the Delaware and Raritan Canal,

87

then to Baltimore by way of the Chesapeake and Delaware Canal. Stop at Annapolis, I think, and then take off for Hampton Roads."

" Quite a trip, Scrimshaw."

Scrimshaw spat again. " I don't know, Davie. Howorth and Stockholm are brave men and good fellows, but they ain't exactly what I'd call seamen. They ain't even good mud pilots, far's I'm concerned. That's why they sent old Scrimshaw along."

" Yep," said Dave dryly.

Scrimshaw looked up at him with a cold eye. " Just because you tried to sink the *Albemarle* singlehanded and got promoted to ' reefer ' don't prove nothing. I mind the time we fished you out of the Atlantic. You wasn't so bigety then, matey."

Dave grinned at his old shipmate. " I can hardly wait to see you sitting beside a launch boiler under a cloud of soot and smoke, trying to look like old Stormalong."

Scrimshaw waved a hand. " I'll suffer," he said gloomily. " I got a message for you from an old shipmate, Davie."

" Who? "

" Acting Midshipman Steven McAllister Raintree."

Dave stared at him. " Steve is a ' reefer ' too? "

" Yup. Pretty soon I'll be the only able seaman left in the whole U.S. Navy, the way they're promoting all you wetnoses. Anyways, Steve says I should tell you, if I see you, that he's looking forward to having you on the *Monticello* again. That boy is sure restless. It'll be a rough day for the Navy when you two lubbers get together."

Chapter 9

MIDSHIPMAN Dave Scott held the tiller of Picket Boat Number One and steered her into the quartering swell of Chesapeake Bay. Now and then a dollop of water flew over the canvas dodger Scrimshaw had rigged over the bow, and splattered the boiler and engine. A skein of smoke rose from the stubby smokestack and drifted to leeward as Sam Higgins stoked the firebox.

Point Lookout lay far behind them, and somewhere in the mistiness about it wallowed Picket Boat Number Two, with a failing engine. Ensign Howorth, in charge of Number One, had decided to press on, thinking too much time had been lost already.

It had been a rugged trip thus far. Both boats had crossed the Lower Bay and had put into New Brunswick, New Jersey, the entrance to the Delaware and Raritan Canal. Here they had stopped for repairs, for Number One had sat on the rocks at Bergen Point while Number Two had been aground nearby on a sandspit. Both launches had been hauled out of the water for repair to their copper bottoms, and for repair to the hole in the bottom and the damaged keel of Number One.

They had taken aboard a pilot at New Brunswick and had left for the Delaware River, reaching Baltimore via the Chesapeake and Delaware Canal. At Baltimore, Dave had seen his father and his aunt and had assured them he was only returning to blockading duty aboard the *Monticello*, for his new mission was a secret one.

On the way south to Annapolis, Number One's engine had failed, and she had been taken in tow by Number Two. The next day they had set out with Number One still in tow. A strong southeast wind had driven them into a harbor on the Eastern Shore, where Number One's engine had been repaired. From there they had run into a southwest wind which forced them into the West River.

The picket boat plunged and wallowed in the cross chop. Scrimshaw came aft and squatted beside David. "Now, Davie, with a spar and a few yards of canvas I could steady this smokejack. She wallows like a tin pot in a little sea like this. I'm beginning to wonder if we'll ever make Albemarle Sound."

Scrimshaw had been right when he had said that Howorth and Stockholm were not seamen. They were willing enough, fine fellows and brave as lions, but the handling of small boats just wasn't in their line.

"God willing," said Scrimshaw gloomily.

They were all filthy dirty and burned by the sun, and the heat of the boiler and the laboring engine hadn't helped much. But Dave was happy. He liked the sea and he liked small boats. He did much of the steering, for the others, with the exception of Scrimshaw, were pretty lubberly at it. They'd let the boat veer and waver so that she'd wallow in the cross chops. None of them had learned how to meet the motion of the boat with the tiller. Dave was like Scrimshaw in his preference for sail, and someone should have thought of rigging the boats temporarily with a standing lug or perhaps a sliding gunter rig, but it was too late now.

Will Cushing was supposed to meet them at Hampton Roads after his leave in his home town of Fredonia, New York. Dave wondered if he had told his widowed mother of the hazardous expedition to which he was committed. She had already lost one heroic son at Gettysburg.

Dave looked astern, hoping to see the telltale thread of smoke that would show that Number Two was following them, but there was nothing to see except the drifting mist and the dingy sails of a fishing boat that was wallowing toward the East Shore. Dave began to have his doubts about Cushing's chances of success. One boat was already having more than its share of troubles, and Dave's boat was laboring along toward Fortress Monroe ready to stop working any minute. But Will Cushing was the kind of man who would paddle up to the *Albemarle* in a canoe and throw rocks at it if he thought he could harm it.

—

Engineer Bill Stotesbury wiped the sweat from his grease-smeared face with a wad of waste and looked at Dave. " I think she's all right now, reefer."

Dave nodded. When they had reached Fortress Monroe, they had been challenged by a patrol boat and then had been towed to the wharf. Ensign Howorth had gone ashore to see if Will Cushing had arrived, to report to him about the missing Number Two, while Scrimshaw had gone to draw rations, coal, and water with Landsmen Lorenzo Deming and Henry Wilkes. Landsman Robert King was busy cleaning up the launch, while Fireman Sam Higgins was cleaning out the fire hole. They were all tired, and drugged from loss of sleep, but there wasn't time to sit around and worry about it.

"Here comes Mister Cushing," said King.

Will Cushing looked pale and drawn. Despite his wiry strength, he suffered a great deal from colds, and it wasn't unusual for him to lose ten pounds in weight every winter. He smiled and waved his hand at the little crew of Number One, and then looked out across the dancing waters of Chesapeake Bay. "No sign of Number Two?" he asked quietly.

"None, sir," said Dave. He had been looking in that direction all morning.

Cushing leaned against a piling. "How is the engine, Stotesbury?" he asked.

"Fine, sir!"

"That's good news in any event. I've arranged for quarters for all of you in the fort."

"Why, sir?" asked Dave.

Cushing made an impatient gesture. "Admiral Lee has been relieved as commander of the North Atlantic Blockading Squadron. Admiral David Porter has taken his place."

"So?" asked Stotesbury.

Cushing grinned wryly. "Admiral Porter has no high opinion of me. He has said more than once that I have more luck than ability. I am to leave here within the hour aboard a tug to look for Number Two."

The men looked at each other. They could see that the young officer was worn thin and tired.

Cushing straightened up. "I wanted to go on with one boat, but the admiral refused to let me."

"Let me go out on the tug, sir!" cried Dave.

Cushing shook his head. "*I* am to go. That's specific."

The officer walked a few steps and then turned. "You're ready for sea, Stotesbury?"

"Yes, sir."

"Good. Get some rest."

They watched him walk slowly toward the fort.

"It's a shame," said Stotesbury.

Sam Higgins spat over the side. "The willing horse does all the work."

"What's the matter with Porter anyway?" asked Landsman King.

"Who knows?" asked Stotesbury. "I know one thing: Mister Cushing isn't well. Why don't they let him alone?"

"There's a war on," said Dave quietly.

They all looked at him.

—

Landsman Henry Wilkes held up his hand. "Hold it!" he yelled excitedly.

Stotesbury reversed the engine, and the launch lost way and then began to move backward. Will Cushing stood up from where he sat beside Dave in the stern sheets. "What is it, Wilkes?"

"The canal is blocked, sir!"

The sluggish waters of the Chesapeake and Albemarle Canal lapped gently alongside the launch. Cushing and Dave made their way forward, leaving Scrimshaw at the tiller. They had left that morning, October 20, from Norfolk, via the canal, to make their way to Albemarle Sound.

Rocks and small-boat hulks had been dumped into the canal. Cushing stared at the obstructions. "We can't get over or around that," he said.

93

Dave shook his head. Cushing's search for the missing Number Two had been fruitless, and Admiral Porter had finally allowed Cushing to proceed toward Albemarle Sound with the one launch. Cushing had a dispatch in his coat pocket from Admiral Porter to W. H. Macomb, commanding the squadron in the North Carolina sounds, to the effect that Cushing be given the additional men he needed to carry out his mission. Porter had added that he had no great confidence in Cushing's success, but he had ordered Macomb to give him all the assistance in his power and to keep boats ready to pick him up if he failed. If Cushing failed, Macomb was ordered to attack the *Albemarle* if and when it appeared and to keep attacking it even if he lost half his vessels.

Will Cushing bit his lip. "We passed a creek two or three miles back that might allow us to circumvent this obstruction. Turn her around, Scrimshaw!"

It was getting warm, and the heat of the boiler made the boat almost impossible to stay in.

Will Cushing drew out his revolver. "Load and prime," he said.

The men picked up their carbines. They checked their Colt revolving pistols and loosened their cutlasses in their sheaths. This was dangerous country, half controlled by roving bands of rebel partisans and militia and half controlled by occasional Union patrol boats.

Wilkes jumped up and thrust up an arm. "Milldam ahead!" he called out.

Dave looked at Cushing. There was no sign of emotion on the young officer's lean face.

Dave looked at the bank. "There's a tidemark, sir," he said. "The water will rise."

Cushing nodded. He slapped Dave on the shoulder. "I'll

make a seaman out of you yet," he promised.

The sun glinted from the brass barrel of the howitzer in the bow as Wilkes slewed the weapon to cover the wooded shore.

Cushing looked at the sky. " About an hour until dusk," he said. " We might make it then."

They sat silently in the boat, watching the tide rise slowly, until Cushing stood up and said: " All right, Stotesbury! Davie, take the tiller."

The launch chugged forward, with David steering for a low place he had noted. As they reached the top of the dam, the rest of the crew jumped over the side and gripped the gunwales to force the heavy craft onward. The bottom scraped and dragged and then plunged into the deeper water on the far side.

" So far, so good," said Cushing. " Slow speed, Stotesbury."

They were only half a mile from the dam when the launch drove hard aground. The weary men went over the side into the knee-deep water and threw their weight and strength into an effort to get the launch afloat again, but it was no use.

Cushing leaned against the side of the launch. " No sense in killing ourselves," he said. " Get some sleep. I'm going ashore to look around. Any volunteers to go along? "

" I'll go, sir," said Dave.

" Count me in too," said Scrimshaw.

They took their carbines and waded ashore. Cushing led the way through the scrub pines.

The wind moaned softly through the woods as they reached a rutted sand road. " Listen! " said Scrimshaw tensely.

They stopped on the road and listened. They could hear

a dog barking from the south.

They padded through the timber and brush until they saw a dim yellow light. " Scout around to the west, Davie," said Cushing. " Scrimshaw, you go east. I'll go straight in. If there are soldiers there, retreat and meet me back at the road."

Dave threaded his way through the brush with his carbine at full cock. The odor of wood smoke came to him. The dog was barking louder now.

Dave saw a ramshackle barn. Beyond it he could make out the creek. There was a low house on the creek bank. A man had come out of the back door, with a shotgun in his hand, and was standing with his back toward Dave, looking to the north.

Dave eased forward and placed the muzzle of his Sharps against the man's back. " Stay where you are," he warned. " Who's in the house? "

" No one."

Dave shoved the carbine forward. He let down the hammer to half cock and then cocked it again. " You're sure? "

The man dropped his shotgun and raised his hands. " Yes! "

Dave whistled softly. Cushing and Scrimshaw came toward him. " Take a look in the house, Scrimshaw," he said.

The dog began to howl. " Quiet, Prince! " said the man.

The dog shut up and went into his kennel. Scrimshaw came out of the house. " No one there," he said.

" Do you have a boat? " asked Cushing of the man.

" Yes, a flatboat."

" Good! We'll borrow it."

They walked down to the creek and got into the flat-boat. Dave urged the man ahead of him. Scrimshaw cast off and poled the flatboat along the quiet creek.

They reached the launch and began to unload the coal into the flatboat. When they had finished, they horsed the howitzer into the flatboat. " Get some sleep," said Cushing. " King, you take first watch, and guard this man."

Dave awoke at dawn. Wilkes was standing guard. They awoke the others, and they all went over the side, including the sullen farmer, and shoved the launch into deeper water. The sun was up by the time they had transferred the coal and the howitzer back into the launch. They poled the flatboat to the farm and left it and the man. He stood on the bank watching them and then shook his fist. " You'll never make it, Yankees! " he yelled.

Scrimshaw placed his right hand under his bewhiskered chin and waggled it as he shook his carbine with his other hand.

They reached the Chesapeake and Albemarle Canal again, this time well past the obstructions. " Clear sailing now," said Scrimshaw.

⁓

It was three days after their experiences at the milldam when Stotesbury stood up on the gunwale and stared ahead. " Patrol boat," he said.

The others looked ahead with reddened eyes. They hadn't seen a soul, friendly or otherwise, in two days. A small side-wheeler was puffing toward them. The Stars and Stripes flew from the jack staff.

" Ahoy, there! " yelled Cushing.

The side-wheeler slowed down, thrashed into reverse, and then coasted easily toward the launch. " What boat is that? " hailed an officer from the bridge.

"Picket Boat Number One, Lieutenant William Cushing, commanding! " called out Wilkes.

"We've been expecting you! How did you get here? "

"Through the canal," said Cushing.

"The canal! Are you mad? Thirty miles of that canal are not guarded by Union forces! Every man who lives along it is a Confederate sympathizer, and there are rebel patrols all along there."

Cushing grinned. "I thought that man who *lent* us his flatboat wasn't too happy! "

"Where are you bound? " called out the officer.

"Roanoke Island," said Cushing.

"Heave them a line," said the officer to a seaman. "We'll be more than pleased to tow you, sir."

The heaving line shot out and was taken by Wilkes. He drew it in and with it the light hawser that had been attached to it. He made it fast around the bitts in the bow of the boat. Stotesbury shut off the hissing, clanking launch engine. "This will be like an excursion up the Hudson to Poughkeepsie," he said with a grin.

The crew dropped into the bottom of the boat as the side-wheeler moved forward, described a wide curve, and started south down the Pasquotank River.

Dave wadded his sea bag under his head and closed his eyes. He was asleep as soon as his head touched the bag.

Chapter 10

WILL CUSHING came down to the wharf at Roanoke Island, the great Union strong point, toward Picket Boat Number One. Dave shook Scrimshaw by the shoulder. " Here comes the skipper, mate," he said.

Scrimshaw opened his eyes and yawned. " 'Bout time," he said.

Cushing dropped into the boat and sat down in the stern sheets. He had a tattered newspaper under his arm, and there was a worried look on his face. " Still no news of Number Two, Davie," he said. He tapped the newspaper. " It seems as if the rebels have heard about our plans, but they haven't learned the correct procedure. Still, they do know we are after her. Someday our government will learn to muzzle the newspapers in regard to military and naval plans. Another thing: There has already been an attempt made to blow up the *Albemarle*."

" *What?* " roared Scrimshaw. He was wide-awake now.

Cushing shoved back his cap. " Early this summer a coal heaver named Charles Baldwin, with four other men, carried two one-hundred-pound torpedoes on stretchers across the swamps behind Plymouth until they reached the bank of the Roanoke River opposite where the ram was moored.

"Baldwin and another man swam across the river upstream of the *Albemarle* and connected the two torpedoes together by a cable. They swam down the river to put the charges on either side of the *Albermarle*'s bow so that they could be exploded from the far bank of the river.

"Guards saw Baldwin, and so Baldwin and his men had to get out of there in a hurry under small-arms fire. That means the rebels will have a closer guard than ever about the ram. It doesn't look good for us."

"We're not quitting, are we, sir?" asked Dave.

Cushing shook his head. "We're supposed to be leaving for Beaufort in the morning with two passengers."

"That's a long way from the *Albemarle*, sir," said Scrimshaw.

Cushing grinned. "Sure it is! But I said, 'We're *supposed* to be leaving.' Actually we'll shove off tonight and go up Albemarle Sound to the squadron blockading Plymouth. There may be spies here, and we want them to think we have gone to Beaufort."

"That's sneaky, sir," said Scrimshaw with a wide grin.

"Round up the crew, Davie," said Cushing. "We'll shove off after dark."

Cushing left the boat to report to headquarters. Scrimshaw patted the torpedo boom. "It won't be long now," he said quietly.

～

The night was dark and misty, with a hint of rain, when Number One cast off from the wharf and steamed out into the choppy waters. The men huddled in their oilskins as the launch pitched and rolled in the chop, with now and then a dash of spray flying over the plunging bow. The engine was working smoothly, for Stotesbury had torn it apart and practically rebuilt it.

They steamed north and then turned west into the sound channel to head toward the squadron. Dave was at the tiller. He knew those waters by day or by night. The only thing that worried him was that Cushing had not said as yet that Dave could go along in the attack on the ram.

There was little talk among the men. Cushing was buried in his thoughts. The only noise was the dashing of the water against the hull, the chuffing of the engine, and the occasional noise as Higgins opened the fire door and shoveled in some coal.

" Lights," said Scrimshaw at long last.

" Union vessels," said Cushing.

A signal lantern shone and began to flick off and on. Cushing took a signal lantern into the bow and signaled back. " It's the *Shamrock*," he said over his shoulder. " Commander Macomb's flagship. We're to make fast to her."

They came alongside and made the launch fast, and Cushing then led the way aboard. The *Shamrock* was the same type of double-ender as the *Sassacus* was but larger.

Dave had heard that Macomb's squadron was composed of the double-enders *Shamrock*, *Otsego*, *Wyalusing*, and *Tacony*; the gunboat *Whitehead*; the tugs *Chicopee*, *Belle*, *Bazley*, and *Valley City*; and the old ferryboat *Commodore Hull*. The squadron was hardly capable of defeating the *Albermarle*, or even of containing it in the Roanoke, but they would try if they had to, and the odds were high against them.

The crew stood on the wet deck while Cushing reported. They could see the dim blue lights of the other vessels through the mist and rain, riding easily at their anchors, with guns shotted and primed, ready to open fire in an instant should the ram appear.

An ensign came out on the deck from the commander's cabin and called for a small boat. " Where away? " asked Ensign Howorth.

The officer turned. " The commander has asked me to go to the other vessels of the squadron to ask for volunteers for an extremely hazardous expedition. I don't know what it's for, do you? "

" Haven't any idea," said Howorth, with his tongue in his cheek.

" There's jamoke in the galley," said the ensign. " You and your men have a mug-up."

It was the next afternoon when Cushing called his crew to the afterdeck. There were six more men with the crew of Number One. Acting Master's Mate John Woodman, of the *Commodore Hull;* Engineer Charles L. Steever, of the *Otsego;* Coal Heaver Richard Hamilton, of the *Shamrock;* Ordinary Seamen William Smith, Bernard Harley, and Edward J. Houghton, all of the *Chicopee.* They had told the crew of Number One that they had all been picked from a much larger number and that some of their mates had offered a month's pay to go along. It was rumored that Will Cushing needed volunteers, and that was enough of an incentive to make almost every man in the squadron want to go along no matter what the expedition was about.

Cushing told them quietly of his plan. He eyed each one of them in turn as he concluded. " You must not expect nor hope to return," he said. " There is nothing but glory, death, or possible promotion to be gained. You will have the satisfaction of getting in a telling blow at the rebels."

Every man stepped forward, with head up.

Cushing nodded in satisfaction. "It would have surprised me to have seen any one of you standing back. We have a day or so to get ready. Mister Howorth will explain the details."

The next morning Cushing beckoned to Dave. Dave got a chance to talk to Cushing alone. They walked forward and stopped by the port paddle-wheel box. "Davie," Cushing said quietly. "I don't want you to go along."

"I volunteered, sir!"

"I know."

"You didn't refuse me then as you should have, sir. Begging the lieutenant's pardon."

Cushing took off his cap and ran a slim hand through his long hair. "Perhaps you're right," he said. He looked out across the river. "I must have more information on that ram and how she is protected. I know of no one who knows this area as well as you do, but I can't let you risk going ashore on a scout. People know you hereabouts. You'd have to go as a civilian. If they catch you, they'll shoot or hang you."

Dave felt his stomach turn over. There was a sour taste at the back of his mouth. He wet his lips. "I'll go, sir."

Cushing rubbed his lean face. "I can't make up my mind, Davie."

Dave leaned forward. "When I enlisted, sir, there were no strings attached to it. I earned my promotion, sir, and I'm hardly younger than the lieutenant was when he joined the Navy as acting master's mate. The lieutenant has no right at all to turn me down if I want to volunteer."

Cushing nodded. " So be it! Now, here's the plan: We leave tonight to go up the river. It's more of a scout and a trial run than the actual attempt. We can drop you off not far from Plymouth. Do you think you can scout the ram and report back no later than tomorrow evening? "

" Yes, sir! "

" I'll send Scrimshaw with you."

Dave shook his head. " With that rolling gait of his and that New England twang to his voice, they'd spot him right away, sir."

" True."

" I'll go in alone."

Cushing looked away. " All right, Davie . . . but if anything happens to you . . . " His voice trailed off and he walked quickly away.

That night at sunset there were heavy clouds on the horizon. The crew of Number One tumbled aboard, with Dave wearing a curious assortment of civilian clothing that had been gathered from the crew of the *Shamrock*. He had concealed a clasp knife, gift of Scrimshaw, and a small revolving pistol inside the roundabout jacket he wore. He didn't feel quite so heroic as the launch was cast off and steamed slowly toward the *Otsego*, which was moored closest to the mouth of the Roanoke River. They picked up the volunteers from the double-ender.

A young officer looked over the rail. " Is it worth ten thousand dollars to you, Cushing, to let me go along? "

Cushing laughed. " Certainly! But you haven't got it." He stood up in the launch. " It's Ensign Gay! I can use another madman or two on this expedition."

Gay swung down the ladder. " Acting Ensign Thomas

Gay reporting, sir. Without doubt the only ten-thousand-dollar ensign in the United States Navy."

The launch chugged toward the river. Dave shook his head. The tide was ebbing. He was sure they had started too late.

Suddenly it seemed as though a giant invisible hand was placed against the bow of the boat. The propeller raced, and Stotesbury shut off the engine.

" We're aground, sir," said Howorth.

Cushing smashed a hand down on the gunwale. " Over the side," he said. " Break her loose."

Time drifted past as the volunteers struggled with the heavy launch. It was two o'clock in the morning before Number One slid into deeper water.

" What now? " asked Ensign Gay.

Cushing peered through the darkness. " We'd best go on," he said. " We won't be able to stand another day of waiting."

They had moved about five hundred yards when a sharp hail rang out across the dark waters. " Who goes there? "

" The Johnnies! " said Cushing. " They can't possibly be down this far! "

A small tug loomed up in the darkness, and the crew could see a howitzer pointed at the launch. " *Who goes there?* " the hail came again. There was no mistaking the Yankee twang.

Cushing stood up. " Lieutenant Cushing and crew, of the U.S.S. *Monticello!* "

" How do we know that? "

" Come aboard and see! "

The tug drew in closer and then was alongside. Two men jumped into the boat. One of them flashed a bull's-eye lantern on Cushing's face and then on the crew. " Tom Gay! " said the officer.

" It's Lieutenant Wilson, sir," said Gay to Cushing.

Dave felt a strong hand grip his shoulder, and he looked up into the freckled face of Steve Raintree. " Shipmate! " he said. " What are *you* doing here? "

Steve grinned. " I might ask the same thing of you, Davie."

" It's young Raintree, sir," said Howorth to Cushing.

Steve turned to Cushing. " I volunteered for duty with this squadron after you left the *Monticello*, sir."

" That figures out," said Cushing dryly.

" We could hear your engine plainly," said Wilson.

Cushing bit his lip. " I was afraid of that. We'll have to have it boxed in."

Wilson climbed back aboard the picket tug. " Come on, reefer," he said to Steve.

Cushing gripped Steve by the shoulder. " Do you know of a place where we can drop off a man without running aground? "

" There is a place about a hundred yards from here where the bank is steep-to. The tide scours out the bottom there. It's about five feet deep."

" Good enough. Will you show us? "

Wilson leaned over the rail. " Go ahead, Raintree," he said.

The launch headed for the shore. Dave stood up. Steve looked at him. " Are they dropping *you* off? "

" Yes."

" Why? "

" I'm to scout the ram."

" *Alone?* "

Dave nodded.

"You need a man with you."

"I can make it."

Steve looked back at the dim outline of the tug. Then he guided Cushing close to the shore. The bow nuzzled the bank. Dave made his way forward and was given a hand up to the bank by Scrimshaw. "See you in Liverpool, mate," he said hoarsely.

The launch went into reverse. She was turned slowly. Suddenly a figure was over the side into the dark waters. The man struck out for the shore. Dave stared at him. He could hear the men in the boat calling out in low voices. The man reached the bank, and Dave dropped onto his belly to grip him by the hand and help him up. "Hello, matey," said Steve Raintree in a cheerful voice. "I made a pierhead jump just to keep you from getting lonely."

Dave stood up. "You crazy fool!"

Steve gripped Dave by the arm. "Let's go! Old Man Wilson will give me a taste of the brig if he catches me."

They hurried into the scrub woods. A cold wind crept over them. Steve kept beating his arms about his wet body. "I'll have to flog the booby all night to keep warm," he said.

Dave stopped. "Go back," he said. "They'll pick you up."

"No!"

"I can't use you. I know these woods and swamps. I can talk like these people. That Yankee accent of yours will surely give you away."

"Will it?" Steve grinned. He lapsed into a perfect imitation of North Carolina speech. "You-all from these here pa'ts, boy?"

Dave couldn't help laughing. Steve was always good for a laugh, and Dave knew his freckled friend had more than his share of courage as well.

"What's the game?" asked Steve.

Dave explained the plan to him.

Steve whistled softly. "And I had to jump into the Roanoke River for a mad thing like that."

"You can always go back, mate."

Steve shook his head. He peeled off his wet midshipman's jacket and buried it under some leaves. He had a gay checked shirt on. "At least my shirt isn't navy," he said. "It was the only clean one I had." He scaled his cap into the brush.

"You'd better get rid of that belt too," said Dave.

Steve took his Navy Colt from its holster. "This won't be of any use until I get it fresh loaded, but I'll keep it for a club." He hid the belt and holster in the brush.

"Let's shove off," said Dave. "It won't be long until daylight. Now listen: We're fishermen. Our boat was taken by the Yankees. We're from the Chowan River area. We're thinking of enlisting in the Confederate Navy to get a berth on the *Albemarle*."

"Aye, aye!"

Dave scratched his chin. "We'll have to have a password in case we get separated in the dark."

"We can use the old Marblehead hail."

"What is it?"

"I call out 'Bodgo!' You answer with 'Molly Waldo!' or visey-versey."

"What does it mean?"

Steve shrugged and thrust out his hands, palms upward. "How should I know? Marbleheaders just use that hail and that answer to recognize each other."

" Bodgo! " said Dave.

" Molly Waldo! "

" Fair enough," said Dave. He started off through the dark woods with Steve close behind him.

Chapter 11

THERE WAS a light pattering of rain on the leaves of the trees. The surface of the river was dappled with the drops. The false dawn was lightening the eastern sky. The hurricane deck of a small steamer showed above the water, and beyond that was an anchored schooner with an artillery piece visible upon her deck.

Dave lay on his belly amongst the wet leaves, peering under a bush. "That must be the *Southfield*," he whispered. "The ship Commander Flusser died on."

Steve's teeth were chattering. "Yup. It's her all right. I've seen her before."

"We knew she had a picket guard on her, but we didn't know about that schooner being anchored here."

"Now we know. We'd better shove off."

"We're about a mile from town."

They backed away from the riverbank and walked toward the road. "I'm still cold," said Steve.

Dave shucked his roundabout coat and handed it to Steve.

"You keep it," said Steve.

"I'm dry; you're wet. Put it on."

"No!"

Dave stopped and faced Steve. "*Put it on!*"

Steve raised his head. "Don't give me orders, mate," he said.

"I'm a full-fledged midshipman. You're an *acting* midshipman. I'm in command!"

For a moment they faced each other as they had on the berth deck of the *Monticello* many months before.

"You heard me," said Dave quietly.

Steve suddenly grinned. "Crinkum-crankum, *Midshipman* Scott. You win."

Steve put on the jacket, and they plodded along the wet road.

Dave suddenly stopped. "Look!" he said tensely.

The *Albemarle* was moored close to the shore, near a wharf. The dark mountain of iron looked inexpressibly formidable as she lay there with the rain running down her rust-marked sides. The gun-port stoppers were closed.

Steve whistled softly. "First time I ever saw her. She's big enough to give any sailor Cape Horn fever."

"Wait until you see her in action, matey."

"I ain't *that* anxious to be a hero!"

Dave studied the big ram in the graying light. Then he noticed something in the water. It was a semicircle of logs barely afloat, with their rounded tops showing slick and shiny, chained together to form a boom defense about the *Albemarle*. This was something Cushing had not reckoned on. "The launch can't get over that boom," he said quietly.

"Maybe we ought to go back now," suggested Steve.

It was a good idea, thought Dave, and he was all for it, but he might gain further information in Plymouth. They had come that far; they could go farther. "No," he said.

"Let's go then."

"You can go back."

"And leave a shipmate? Bodgo!"

"Molly Waldo!" said Dave. "I'll go ahead. You wait half an hour and then come in. Keep away from me. Even if you see me, don't talk to me. Learn all you can. I'll meet you back here about noontime."

Dave walked down the road. He could see earthworks near the riverbank. A squad of soldiers marched toward one of them. The streets of the town were empty. The rain pattered down on the drab houses. A wraith of smoke hung over the barracks near the river.

Dave walked down to the riverbank and out onto a wharf. He could see the ram plainly. The log boom completely encircled it. There were piles of firewood on the bank, covered by canvas to keep them dry. He knew they would be lighted at night if an attack came against the ram. The ram was moored at the upriver end of the town, so that an attacking force would have to run the gantlet of shore batteries and heavy rifle fire. Sentries paced along the shore, huddled under strips of canvas that they wore over their heads and shoulders.

There were piles of coal near the wharves, and Dave was sure they were part of the stores captured by the rebels when Plymouth had been recaptured by them with the help of the *Albemarle* in April.

He walked along the river front to get a closer look at the ram. A sentry stepped out of a shelter. "Git, sonny!" he said.

Dave bent his shoulders forward and peered half-wittedly at the sentry. "She's a whopper," he said with an ingratiating grin. "Near as big as Grandpa's barn back home."

" Git! "

Dave shuffled off until he reached the end of the wharf area. It was full daylight now. Soldiers walked up and down the muddy streets. They were a poor-looking lot. Thin little men for the most part, with some of them hardly more than boys, and others graybeards. Conscripts or militia, thought Dave. They wore threadbare butternut-colored uniforms, and many of them were barefooted.

He saw a familiar-looking thatch of straw-colored hair. It was Steve Raintree, talking to a gaunt-looking sergeant. They walked toward the barracks, with Steve talking volubly. Trust him to find out how many troops were there and where they were situated.

Dave stepped into a doorway and lounged there, whittling at a piece of wood. There were plenty of soldiers there all right, and even if they were second-rate troops, they could pepper an open launch in the river.

Steve was out of sight; so Dave wandered off toward the outskirts of the town. There was a fort situated there. It had been Fort Williams when the Union forces had held the town. Cannon peered from the embrasures, and the rebel flag hung soggily in the damp air. The rain had stopped, and the sun was trying to come out.

He knew there was another fort, once named Fort Wessells after the former Union commander of the troops there. So he walked out toward Welch's Creek and saw former Fort Wessells. It seemed to be well garrisoned, but as at the other fort the troops were a seedy-looking, half-disciplined appearing lot.

He headed for the river again to look at the *Albemarle*. Her flag hung from her mast, and sentries stood on the upper deck. Dave had thoughts of waiting until darkness and sending Steve to warn Cushing about the log boom while he, Dave, would wait his chance and swim out to cut the boom loose. He walked back toward the center of town. A platoon of troops marched by in the mud.

Dave looked for Steve, but the freckle-faced middie was not to be seen. An officer came out of a building from which hung a flag. He yawned and looked up and down the street. Then he looked toward Dave. A wave of fear crept over Dave, and his insides seemed to turn to mush. He recognized the filthy shell jacket and the battered slouch hat with the bedraggled feather in it. He started to walk toward the river.

" Hey, you! " yelled Cap'n Rance.

Dave walked faster, past a group of curious soldiers.

" Stop that boy! " yelled Rance.

Dave sprinted toward the river, cut around a sagging warehouse, and ran along the riverbank quite near the huge ram.

Rance rounded the corner. " Halt or I fiah! " he yelled.

Dave ran on, with head down. A pistol cracked, and he heard the hum of the bullet. He looked back.

" Stop that boy! " roared Rance.

Dave turned in time to see a lean soldier standing right in front of him with his rifle held up, butt toward Dave. He knew he was going to be hit and threw up an arm. The steel-shod butt drove his arm aside and caught Dave full on the forehead, smashing him back against a building. The last thing he remembered was seeing the tobacco-stained teeth of the grinning soldier.

~

Water splashed over Dave. He opened his eyes to look up into the sneering face of Cap'n Rance. " Well, well,

well," said Rance. He threw the water bucket into a corner of the cell. "The Yankee-loving chicken has come home to roost!"

Two soldiers lounged behind Rance, leaning on their rifles. Rance turned. "Yuh see this scar on my chin? This Yankee puppy done that in Wilmington months ago when he and his Yankee pappy was escaping from conscription."

"Sure don't he'p yore looks any, Cap'n Rance," said one of the men with a wide grin.

"Shut up!" Rance turned to look down at Dave. "What yuh doin' here?"

Dave sat up and felt his aching head. "Come to get a job," he said.

"So? Where yuh been all these months?"

"My father was pilot on the *Phantom*. I was washed overboard in the Western Bar Channel and picked up by a picket boat from Fort Caswell."

"Yeh? So where yuh been since then?"

"Working here and there."

"Here and there? *Where?*"

Dave shrugged. "Near Green Swamp and other places."

Rance took Dave's clasp knife and pistol from his pocket. "What are these fer?"

"I always had that knife. I found the pistol."

Rance turned the knife. The brass letters U.S.N. had been fastened to one side. "Yeh? A Yankee Navy knife?"

"It was my father's knife. He gave it to me."

Rance nodded. "Sure, sure . . ." He turned the knife over. The letters U.S.S. *Monticello* had been carved into the bone side. "U.S.S. *Monticello*," sneered Rance. "I happen to know she wasn't in the Navy befo' the wah. I also happen to know she's part of the North Atlantic

Blockading Squadron off Cape Feah."

Dave wet his lips. It was Scrimshaw's knife. " Well," he said quickly, " I was wrong. I found the knife, and the pistol was my father's."

Rance scratched in his unkempt whiskers. " Sho? Now am I supposed to believe that whopper? "

" You can do what you like, Rance."

The man moved swiftly. A boot toe caught Dave under the left ribs. He grunted in pain. " *Cap'n* Rance! " snapped the provost.

" *Captain* Rance," repeated Dave.

" That's bettah! Now we happen to know theah was a Yankee picket tug and a launch foolin' around neah the mouth of the Roanoke last night. Yuh know anything about thet? "

" No."

The boot toe thudded against Dave's side again. " Youah sure? "

" Let the kid alone, Rance," said one of the men.

" I'm in command heah! "

" Yeh, yeh, but the kid ain't done nothin'."

Rance eyed Dave suspiciously. " I'm goin' to tell the cunnel about yuh, Yankee. If we think youah a spy, youah goin' to have a drumhead court-martial and get shot, or mebbe hung."

Dave stood up. " I was only looking for a job."

" We-uns will give yuh a job. Yuh kin take a walk up Ladder Lane and down Rope Street, sonny." Rance tilted his head to one side, raised his left arm, and jerked it upward as though pulling on a rope, while he goggled his little eyes and thrust out his tongue. He grinned as he walked to the door. " I only wish that Yankee pappy of youahs was heah to go along with yuh!"

They closed and locked the door. Dave felt his side and then his head. Of all the luck to have run into Cap'n Rance again.

—

The long afternoon had dragged by on leaden feet. It was getting dusk. Dave stood at his cell window and looked out toward the huge ram that seemed to squat on the surface of the Roanoke like some prehistoric monster.

A soldier rounded the corner, carrying a long flintlock rifle at right shoulder shift. He wore a threadbare butternut uniform and a tattered slouch hat from which tufts of straw-colored hair protruded like unshocked wheat. Dave stared at the soldier. It was Steve Raintree.

Steve halted near the wooden-barred window of the cell. "Private Steven Treerain," he said. "Captain Buscombe's Independent Militia Company of Noth Caholina Infantry, suh!"

"Steve, you've gone mad!"

Steve grinned. "Nope. I got all the information on the troops here and was ready to leave when I heard you were in the brig. I signed up right then and there, figuring it would take some time to get me into uniform, but they ain't fooling around. They need the halt, the lame, and the blind in this milishy outfit. So here I am! What do I do?"

"Get out of that rebel suit and get back to Lieutenant Cushing. Tell him all you know."

"Without you, shipmate?"

"*Without me!*"

Steve shook his head. "'A messmate before a shipmate,

117

a shipmate before a stranger, a stranger before a dog, but a dog before a " sojer." ' "

" Haul out of here, I say! "

" You ain't in any position to give orders to me, reefer." Steve looked up and down the street, and then he handed Dave a bowie knife. " Swiped that from the sergeant. Get to cutting. I'll be back in an hour or so."

Steve vanished down the street.

Dave walked to the door and listened. He could hear the slapping of cards and the laughing of the guards as they played.

He tested the edge of the knife on his thumb and drew blood. The bars were of exceptionally hard wood and set close together. He worked steadily, with sweat greasing his shaking hands. As he cut through each bar, he plastered the cut with mud from the damp floor of the cell. It was dark outside now. It wouldn't be long before Cushing would make his attempt, and if he didn't know what to expect, he would certainly fail and possibly lose his life and the lives of his crew.

He cut through the last bar and turned quickly as he heard boots grating on the filthy floor of the hall outside. He slid the knife under the thin blanket on the cot, wiped his hands on his shirt, and sat down atop the knife.

The door was unlocked and swung open. Rance came in. " The cunnel says he'll question yuh."

" Now? "

" In the mawnin'."

Dave felt relief.

Rance leaned against the wall. He took out his pistol and slapped the heavy barrel against the palm of his left hand. " But I know how yuh Yankees kin lie. I figger I kin warm yuh up a little for the cunnel."

Dave stood up.

Rance grinned. " Wheah's youah old man? "

" I don't know."

" Wheah did he go on the *Phantom*? "

" To Halifax, I think."

" Close to Yankeeland, eh? "

" I wouldn't know."

The barrel was hitting harder now. Rance leaned forward. " Come awn now! Just what are yuh doin' heah in Plymouth? "

" Looking for a job."

Rance swung the heavy pistol, but Dave jumped to one side. He snatched up the empty water bucket and swung it with all his strength. It crashed down on Rance's head, driving him to the floor. Dave picked up the pistol, jumped up on the cot, and pushed at the bars. Three of them fell out into the street.

" Cap'n Rance! " called out a guard. " Yuh all right? "

Dave pushed out two more bars and thrust his head and shoulders through the window. He pulled hard with his arms and fell headlong into the street. He looked up to see a pair of sturdy legs clad in butternut-colored cloth. He raised the pistol.

" Take it easy! " said Steve. " Break for the river! "

Dave ran toward the river.

A guard thrust his head from the window. " Hey, you! " he yelled at Steve. " Yuh see that Yankee boy? "

" He ran toward the center of town," said Steve.

The guard vanished. Steve hurled his ancient rifle into a shed, peeled off his coat and hat, and ran after Dave. It was raining lightly again.

They dashed down the riverside. Men yelled from behind them. There was a rickety wharf sagging down toward the water. A leaky skiff was moored to it. Dave jumped into it, and Steve was close behind him. Steve cut the painter loose. " Shove off! " he snapped.

" All gone, sir! " said Dave cheerily as he heaved against a rotting piling. They slipped out into the current. Dave shipped the warped oars and began to pull steadily. A rifle cracked flatly from the bank, and the slug smacked through the side of the skiff.

Then they were out in the center of the river, with the rain suddenly driving down hard. " A real Irish hurricane," said Steve cheerfully.

The lights of the town drifted astern as Dave pulled hard, helped by the current. They would have to pass the *Southfield* and the moored schooner before too long.

Steve looked ahead. " I see a glim," he said.

" The picket boats," said Dave. His head ached, and he had scraped a shoulder coming through the window, but he felt a lot better, despite the precarious situation they were still in.

The rain sheeted down, and they could hardly see the dim shore.

" There they are! " said Steve.

Dave looked over his shoulder. He could see the low hulk of the *Southfield* and the schooner beyond it. He turned the boat toward the far shore, and they shot toward the boats. There was no one on the deck of the sunken Union boat, but a rifleman was watching them from the schooner. " Who goes there? " he called out.

" Fishermen," said Steve.

" This time of night? "

"Yup," said Steve.

"Yuh won't catch nothin' down theah but a Yankee or two."

"Good, we-uns will bring one back for yuh."

They passed the schooner. "This skiff is taking water fast," said Steve. "Too fast . . . "

"Man the pumps!"

"It ain't funny."

"Can you swim any better?"

Steve shrugged. "Not much better, but I have a pig tattooed on my foot. Taffy Brown says that'll save you from drowning."

Water lapped over the side of the craft. "Here's your chance to prove whether he's right or not," said Dave. He cast off his shoes and rolled into the water, followed by Steve. They clung to the water-filled skiff. It drifted toward the shore and soon Dave felt the soft bottom under his feet. They crawled ashore on the opposite bank from which they had come.

"Now what?" asked Steve gloomily.

Dave looked over his shoulder at the forbidding swamp behind them. "It's a long way to the river mouth," he said.

"That's cheering."

They squatted on the soaked ground. Dave began to shiver. "Looks like we go upriver again to see if we can find another skiff."

"Why up? We'll have to pass the *Southfield* again."

"Have you any better idea?"

Steve shook his head. "Let's go. I've been wet so many times since I joined you that I think I'm getting webs between my toes."

They plodded up the mushy bank and faded into the

121

woods when they saw the schooner and the *Southfield.* Soon they were up to their knees in a wet wilderness of mud, briers, and scrub trees. They floundered on and on until they could see lights from across the river. " Plymouth," said Steve.

They hunted the riverbank for a boat, and all they found was the rotting hulk of a corn barge. It was getting late. Cushing would soon be coming up the Roanoke to make his attempt. They had to warn him about the log boom.

" Back we go," said Dave.

Steve wiped the muck from his hands. " One thing I like about you, Davie, is that you never quit."

" Bodgo! "

" Molly Waldo! "

They plodded down-river again through the clinging muck and briers.

Chapter 12

THE GREAT low trees hung over the dark waters of the Roanoke, obscuring the sky and thickening the darkness. A dog howled mournfully from inland. Steve Raintree shivered. " Who wouldn't sell a farm and go to sea? " he asked.

Dave stopped and leaned against a tree. They were both soaked to the skin and torn by briers and brush. Dave wasn't quite sure where they were. Steve had told him there were about four thousand troops in the vicinity of Plymouth, on both sides of the Roanoke, and it would be easy enough to stumble into one of their camps or into a patrol.

" There's the schooner," said Steve suddenly.

Dave stared into the darkness. Now and then a spit of rain touched his face, blown by the light south wind. Then he made out the dim outline of the schooner. There was a faint splash of yellow light from an opened door, and then it was gone as quickly as it had come. But the dim glow had shown Dave the sunken hulk of the *Southfield* beyond the guard schooner.

" How far are we from the river mouth? " asked Steve.

"Maybe six miles."

"What do we do? Go down there or stay here?"

Dave wiped the rain from his face. They were both tired, and they would have to flounder along through the muck, wading the tidal streams and avoiding prowling rebels. Dave thought fast. "If the launch gets past the schooner and the *Southfield*, she'll strike for the ram. If she can't get past them, she'll *have* to go back."

"So?"

"There's no sense in our killing ourselves in this swamp. If Cushing goes back, we'll go back too. Maybe we can hail him and get a ride."

Steve shrugged. "Oh, I'm getting used to walking in water up to my waist, Davie. *I* don't mind walking."

"But if she does get past the schooner, we'll have to get aboard the launch and tell Cushing about the log boom."

"Maybe we ought to tell him before he reaches the schooner."

Dave shook his head. "If the guard sees him, they'll know something is up. The whole river-front garrison will be alert. Besides, you know very well if Cushing gets past the schooner, *nothing* will turn him back, log boom or no, but it's up to us to warn him about it in any case."

"Aye, aye!"

"Then we wait here."

Steve shivered. "I'll scout around, matey. Ain't no use standing in this drizzle until Cushing gets here."

Steve vanished into the brush.

Dave stood under a tree. His body ached where Cap'n Rance had kicked him. Dave had felled the provost twice now, and Rance would never let him get away with anything like that again if he got his hands on Dave.

Shortly after, Steve came out of the brush like a dripping otter. "We're in luck," he said hoarsely. "There's a shack back away."

They threaded their way through the darkness until they were fifty yards from the river. A small shack stood in a little clearing. It sagged precariously, and the door hung loose on leather hinges. They went inside and felt their way about. There was a broken-down bunk in one corner filled with cornhusks. A tattered blanket lay atop the husks.

Steve prodded the cornhusks. "A real donkey's breakfast," he said.

Dave could hear Steve's teeth chattering. "Hop in," he said. "I'll stand guard near the river. You can spell me after a time."

Steve handed Dave the blanket. "I'll burrow into the husks," he said. "You take the blanket."

Dave left the shack and draped the musty blanket about his shoulders. It wasn't much protection, but it was better than nothing at all.

—

A hand shook Dave awake. He looked into the pale face of Steve. "Show a leg!" said Steve. "Do you hear the news there, sleeper?"

It seemed to Dave that he had hardly fallen to sleep after his cold, wet watch on the river front, but he knew Steve had probably done more than his allotted time of standing out there in the wet woods.

Dave sat up. "Any sign of them?"

"Nary a one."

"Wonder what time it is?"

"I figure they stand two-hour watches on the schooner.

I can tell when they change guards. They changed twice since you went asleep."

Dave jumped to his feet. " It must be well after midnight then! "

" Yup."

Dave took the damp blanket from Steve. " Hit the sack," he said.

" Maybe I'd better watch with you."

" You've done more than your share, mate. I'll let you know if anything happens."

Steve dropped into the bunk and worked his way down into the husks. His head dropped, and he was off to sleep almost at once.

Dave plodded to the riverbank. Maybe Cushing wasn't coming after all.

He peered through the dimness toward the schooner. There wasn't a sign of life aboard her, but the guard was probably composed of North Carolina boys who were born hunters, with keen ears and eyes.

Then Dave seemed to feel, rather than hear, something else in the down-river darkness. He edged his way to the brink of the river.

There was something dark moving in the water, closer and closer to the schooner; then it moved farther away from the schooner and toward the other bank, to pass between the schooner and the *Southfield*. The wind shifted a little, and Dave heard the faint, muffled beating of an engine. *It was Cushing!*

There was no time to alert Steve. The launch was moving steadily upriver. Dave threw the blanket aside and waded into the cold water. He struck out strongly, fighting the current. He was midway across the river when he heard the soft sound of voices aboard the schooner, and then he saw a spurt of flame from a match, momentarily lighting a bearded face.

Dave passed the bow of the schooner and saw two dim shapes ahead of him: two boats, moving slowly against the current. He saw the short smokestack of the lead boat and the thin outline of the torpedo stanchion, and he knew he was back with his shipmates at last.

"Ahoy, Number One!" he called out softly.

The launch slowed down.

"Ahoy!" said Dave desperately. Then he tried the challenge Steve had taught him. "Bodgo!"

"Molly Waldo!" said a familiar voice. It was Scrimshaw.

A hand gripped Dave by the left arm, and willing hands hauled him into the boat. Dave looked up into the lean face of Will Cushing. "You spend a lot of time getting fished out of cold water, reefer," he said dryly.

The *Southfield* was a dim shape astern, and then the launch was around a bend in the river. A rowing cutter was being towed by the launch, and Dave could see that it was filled with armed men.

"There's a log boom about the *Albemarle*," gasped Dave.

"What's that?" demanded Cushing.

Dave explained as quickly as he could. For a moment Cushing stood there in the darkness staring upriver as though he would pierce the veil with his eyes. "We could land at a wharf downstream from the ram," he said, "and then attack the ram from the shore. I've got a load of tough salts with me in the cutter. We're all heavily armed and willing to tackle twice our number. We could board the *Albemarle,* cut her hawsers, and drift downstream, *if* we could get through that boom."

Dave shook his head. "It's lashed and chained, with stout logs forming it. You'd never get away with it, sir. Besides, there are thousands of troops in the town and the forts near it."

"By grab," said Scrimshaw, "if we could get her loose and down the river, we could start her engines and steam out into the bay with the Stars and Stripes flyin' in the morning breeze! "

"We haven't got a flag," said Higgins.

Cushing grinned. "Who says so? We've got one all right! "

The launch moved slowly up the river, with Cushing in the bow. The water gurgled loudly past the cutwater, and the muffled beating of the engine seemed too loud to Dave. Cushing was in his so-called harness. There were five signal lines to be controlled by him. Ensign Gay, who would handle the torpedo boom had a line attached to his wrist, the other end of which was held by Cushing. The boom would be moved forward when the line was pulled.

Another line held by Cushing was tied to Engineer Stotesbury's ankle. A single pull on it meant Stotesbury should increase speed; two pulls meant he should stop the engine. Another line was attached to the brass howitzer that Ensign Howorth would man at the last possible moment, attaching the line to himself to receive his signals.

The three lines were in Cushing's right hand. In his left hand he held the two lines to control the torpedo after it had been lowered from the boom. One line was to detach it from the boom and allow it to float upward beneath the ram; the other line was to release the firing pin and explode the torpedo.

128

Dave wondered how Cushing would be able to think of which line to pull at which time. It would take a man with nerves of ice to do it, and do it right.

"There's Plymouth," said Dave suddenly as the launch chuffed around a bend.

The ram was dimly visible, a square-looking silhouette in the darkness at the far end of the town.

Cushing gave the wheel a quick turn and headed in for the bank. There was a wharf there. *No*, thought Dave, Cushing would never get the ram past the log boom.

The silence was broken by the sharp barking of a dog near the wharf. "Who goes there?" called out a voice from the great ram.

Cushing sheered off. The time was past for boarding. He gave the engineer's line a hard pull, and instantly the launch surged forward at full speed.

"Who's there? *Who goes there?*" roared the sentry.

"Ahead fast!" commanded Cushing. He turned to look astern toward the cutter towed by the launch. "Cast off, Peterkin!" he yelled. "Go back and take care of those pickets on the schooner!"

The line was cast off and the launch shot forward, relieved of the heavy drag of the cutter. The engine chugged steadily. Then aboard the ram they heard the hard strident noise of a battle rattle as it was sprung, alerting the crew of the huge ram. It sounded as though a giant had run the length of a big picket fence, dragging a stick across the palings.

They raced toward the *Albemarle*. Rifles began to flash in the darkness. "Who goes there? Who goes there?" called out the guards aboard the ram.

"The boom!" called out Dave to Cushing. "*Don't forget the boom!*"

The logs were but twenty yards away when a huge fire sprang up suddenly on the shore. It was the pile of firewood Dave had seen that very day, and it had been soaked with turpentine. Leaping shadows showed up on the hulk of the ram, only to disappear and reappear at another place. The log boom was plainly visible now, and Cushing steered in close, coolly eyed it, then sheered off away from the ram.

"We're not retreating, sir?" demanded Howorth in dismay.

Cushing's answer was typical of the man. "Full speed!" he yelled.

Bullets pocked the water as the launch gained speed. Rifles crackled like popcorn in a gigantic skillet, and there were sounds overhead as though partridges had taken flight as bullets whispered through the air.

Cushing spun the steering wheel, and the heavy launch heeled over as she turned to head directly for the *Albemarle*.

Scrimshaw handed Dave a Sharps carbine. He was actually grinning as he looked at the ram. "Ain't she as big as the old *Courser*, Stormalong's packet!" he said.

They were close now. A guard fired a shotgun, and the charge whistled past Dave and tore the back out of Cushing's coat. He dropped three of his lines and stood there perfectly calm as they surged toward the slimy log barricade.

Dave fired the carbine and saw a guard drop his rifle and grip his left arm. Scrimshaw spat over the side and fired his carbine.

Men were racing down toward the riverbank, flourishing their rifles. The flames leaped higher and higher, and

130

smoke drifted toward the launch. Then the firing died away for some inexplicable reason. A marksman stood up on the upper deck of the ram and aimed at Cushing. Dave snatched up a carbine, cocked it, and fired it almost in one fluid motion. The slug sang off the barrel of the guard's rifle, and he dropped it.

"Thanks, Davie!" said Cushing cheerily. He was actually smiling.

The launch engine was pounding away with a full head of steam. The crew stared fascinated at the log boom and then at the wet bulk of the ram.

"What boat is that?" yelled a man on the *Albemarle*.

"Cleopatra's Barge!" sang out John Woodman.

Cushing raised his head. "We'll soon let you know what boat this is, Johnny Reb!" called he.

Cushing gave an order to Ensign Gay. Gay swiftly swung the boom around. Cushing leaned over and yanked the firing lanyard of the howitzer. A double dose of canister glanced from the *Albemarle* and smashed into the men standing near the fire on the shore.

The bow struck something hard. There was a ripping, tearing sound as the bow rose and the launch quivered under the driving of the engine. Cushing swayed and stumbled but did not fall. The hiss of escaping steam came from the boiler. There they were and there they would stay.

Dave looked up at the towering black side of the ram, and it seemed bigger and more formidable than ever. His heart thudded against his ribs in time to the laboring engine.

The boom was full forward by now, and the winch in the bottom of the launch began to grind as the boom was lowered. A gun-port stopper dropped and the snout of one of the ram's eight-inch Brooke rifles peered out. Dave shuddered as he looked into the black maw of the big gun. He could see the gun crew behind it. Twenty seconds to fire, estimated Dave. His skin seemed to crawl, and a ball of ice formed in the pit of his stomach.

The torpedo was fully submerged now. Dave glanced at Will Cushing. There was no emotion on the officer's face. Cushing pulled his right-hand line to release the torpedo. "One! Two! Three! Four! *Five!*" he chanted. He jerked as a bullet ripped at his collar and another at his sleeve, while two more flicked through the slack of his coat. It seemed incredible that he should stand there untouched within point-blank range of the guards.

Slowly Cushing pulled the firing-pin line.

There was a muffled roar from beneath the *Albemarle*. Water spouted up the side of the ram at just the same time as the eight-inch gun blasted flame and smoke toward the launch. But the gun could not be depressed low enough, and most of the charge hurtled over the launch and splashed harmlessly into the river. The shock of the explosion and the firing of the gun had formed a huge wave that dashed against the launch and flattened it as though it had been made of wet pasteboard. Now there was no chance to take the launch off the boom.

Dave was hurled back against the boiler and then against the side of the boat.

There was a brooding silence after the gun fired. "Surrender or we'll blow you out of the water!" yelled the gun-crew captain.

Rifles began to flash again. Bullets cut into the boat and sang from the metal boiler. Cushing's left hand was bleeding.

" Surrender! "

" Never! " roared Cushing. He took off his sword, revolver, and coat. He coolly sat down and pulled off his shoes as bullets sang past him. " Men! " he yelled. "*Save yourselves!* " He stood up and dived cleanly into the dark waters.

Dave was yanked to his feet by Scrimshaw. " Over with ye, lad! " he cried. He literally threw Dave into the cold Roanoke and then jumped in after him.

Other members of the crew struck the water. The firelight danced on the little waves. Dave struck out to get past the circle of light thrown by the roaring fire. Then he was in semidarkness, with Scrimshaw splashing along behind him and making heavy weather of it.

Dave looked back as he fought against the current. He wasn't sure, but it seemed to him she was listing a little. The launch was afloat, and some of the crew were still in it. Then Dave looked at Scrimshaw. The old salt was gasping for breath. " Can you make it? " asked Dave.

Scrimshaw nodded. " I got a pig tattooed on me left foot and some salt in me pocket. 'Tis to save me from drowning and for good luck, lad."

Dave looked down-river. He thought he saw the rowing cutter, but a sudden dash of rain cut off his view. Then it seemed as though he was again in the cold ocean far off Cape Fear, as he had been when he had been washed overboard from the *Phantom,* for he could see neither shore as the current swept him and Scrimshaw out of sight of the ram.

Scrimshaw groaned. " Go ye on, mate! " he said.

" No! "

Dave gripped Scrimshaw by the loose collar of his blouse and tried to tow him, but the man was too heavy and Dave's clothing was pulling him down.

"Go on!" said Scrimshaw.

It was a temptation. Dave was tiring fast, and he didn't think he could make the shore himself, and then he thought of the old Navy saying: "A messmate before a shipmate, a shipmate before a stranger, a stranger before a dog, but a dog before a ' sojer.' " Dave gripped tighter to Scrimshaw's collar and swam with all his remaining strength through the darkness until his feet hit the muddy bottom of the Roanoke.

Scrimshaw gasped. "I'm done," he said weakly.

"Put your big feet down, mate," said Dave.

"I'll drown!"

"Put your feet down, I said!"

Scrimshaw sank a little, and then a beautiful smile came across his homely face. "I never thought I'd love land so much, muddy as it is, Davie."

They waded ashore and dropped on the wet ground. Dave felt sick and weak. He dropped his head into the mud and lay still, listening to the pattering of the rain against the leaves of the low trees.

Chapter 13

T HE HARD HAND gripped Dave by the nape of the neck. "Quiet!" snapped Scrimshaw. "Listen!"

Dave opened his eyes. There was a pale watery-looking light in the eastern sky, and he knew then they were on the western shore of the Roanoke.

Scrimshaw jerked his thumb toward a clump of wet brush, and the two of them crawled into its cover. They lay there listening. Something rustled in the brush inland, and there was a soft sucking sound as if someone was walking slowly through the clinging mud.

Scrimshaw closed his right hand on a thick branch that lay beside him.

The brush rustled again, and Dave saw a dim figure coming toward them. Scrimshaw made a pincers with the thumb and forefinger of his left hand. Dave nodded. They would close in on the intruder from both sides. Scrimshaw touched his lips with his left hand and then gripped his throat. They were to prevent any outcry.

The sucking noise came again. Dave bellied away from Scrimshaw and slid under a bush. The man came toward them and was just between them in the dimness when

Scrimshaw whistled softly. Dave got to his feet and plunged forward with outstretched arms, catching the stranger about the waist and driving him hard toward Scrimshaw. The old sailor slipped in the mud, and the stranger was driven against Scrimshaw, knocking him against a tree. Scrimshaw raised his club.

"Bodgo!" gasped the intruder.

"Molly Waldo!" said Dave.

It was Steve Raintree. Dave stared at him and laughed. The young midshipman wore a battered straw hat and had the musty blanket, poncho fashion, about his shoulders, with his head through a hole in it. His freckled face was smeared with mud.

Scrimshaw rubbed his middle. "I thought ye was to get *him*, not me, Davie," he said.

"Where'd you go, Davie?" asked Steve.

Dave explained what had happened. Steve nodded. "I calculated that was where you went."

"The only thing we don't know is what happened to Cushing and whether or not the ram was actually sunk," said Dave.

"I haven't seen Mister Cushing or any of the rest of them," said Steve. "I started inland, looking for a road, about an hour ago and ran into an old Negro. He told that there had been a whopping big explosion at Plymouth and that some Yankee sailors had been captured there. He said he didn't know whether or not the *Albemarle* had been sunk."

Dave looked at Scrimshaw. The old sailor scratched in his beard. "Would take a big hole to sink that ram," said Scrimshaw.

"The Negro told me the woods were full of soldiers

136

looking for us. On both sides of the river they're swarming like mad hornets."

Scrimshaw scratched more vigorously. "That's what I figgered. Where are we, Davie?"

"The Middle River is westerly of us. It runs into the Roanoke some miles down-river. We're on a sort of peninsula between both rivers. Down-river, on the other bank, is Eastmost River, which flows into Batchelor's Bay. The Roanoke trends east this side of Eastmost River and then flows into Batchelor's Bay too. It's mostly cypress swamp country, more water than land. Our best bet is to cross the Roanoke if we can, and work down the far bank to the mouth of the Roanoke."

"Just like that," said Steve dryly.

Scrimshaw hitched up his wet trousers. "I'm for it, mates. I don't hanker to sit out the rest of the war in a reb prison."

"Yup," said Steve. "Only that won't be so bad for you, Scrimshaw. If they catch us, they'll shoot us or hang us — Davie for being a spy and me for being a deserter from Cap'n Buscombe's Independent Militia Company of North Carolina Infantry."

"I always thought ye'd join the rebels if ye had the chance, matey."

"Listen!" said Dave.

Behind them, somewhere in the thick woods, they could hear the barking of a dog and the shouting of men.

"Them ain't no Yankees yelling," said Scrimshaw soberly.

The eastern sky was fairly alight with the coming of the false dawn. Dave had once heard bloodhounds baying along the Chowan River, hunting down an escaped slave,

137

and the sound had haunted him for years. Now he knew how the desperate slave must have felt as he plunged through the swamps with very little hope of escaping.

Steve looked toward the river. " That skiff we escaped from Plymouth in is upriver apiece. Maybe we can caulk her up enough to get across the river before the sun comes up."

The three of them forced their way through the clinging briars until they saw the water-filled skiff close to the shore. They horsed the skiff to the shore and shook it from side to side until most of the water was out of it; then they turned it over and emptied the remainder of the water out of it. " Crinkum-crankum," said Steve. " A lobster basket would make a better craft."

" Can we fix it? " asked Dave dubiously.

Scrimshaw spat. " Jack Tar is a handy man, matey." He stripped off his wet undershirt and tore it into long shreds. " Steve, go ye and find some boards to make paddles. Davie, you scout them woods. Old Scrimshaw will make this skiff was all a-taunto in less time than it takes to get a mug-up of jamoke."

" Jamoke, he says," groaned Steve, " and me freezing to death! "

" Shake a leg there, matey! " snapped Scrimshaw.

The two middies walked into the woods while Scrimshaw set to work. Dave headed west through the swamp. He could hear the barking of the dogs, but the sound seemed to be more toward the north.

He came out onto a rutted road, hardly more than a winding trail through the woods. The wind whispered through the wet trees. It brought thoughts of courageous Will Cushing and the equally courageous men who had served as crew aboard Picket Board Number One. Some of them must have been captured, while others must have been killed or drowned in the cold waters of the Roanoke.

Suddenly he heard the doleful howling of a bloodhound from the south. That placed searching parties to north and south. Then the wind shifted, and he heard the faint mumbling of voices to the west. He faded into the underbrush and crouched in the thick muck.

"How many you figger got away, Clay?" a man called out.

"That officer was one, Dan. There was some others got into the watah too. One of them drownded, that we know for sure. They found his body just south of town."

Dave felt his heart beating like a tom-tom. Then two men came out of the brush and stood there looking up and down the road. They wore faded and muddy butternut-colored uniforms and carried long rifles.

"Listen to them hounds," said the taller of the two soldiers.

"Sounds like music to me, Clay. Them Yankees in the swamp must be sweatin' blood 'bout now."

Clay nodded. "Still," he said reflectively, "them Yankee sailors was the bravest men I ever seen. Yuh see that officer standing there in that launch working them lines? He had to explode that torpedo with Minié balls whistling past his ears and cutting through his uniform."

Dan nodded. "Never thought much of Yankees till then. In a way I almost wish they'd git away."

Clay shook his head. "Cap'n Rance says he aims to git all of them, 'specially thet youngun, the one he says was a spy."

"Yeh, him and his spies!"

"We'd best keep lookin'. Old Rance ain't in what I'd call a good mood."

"Where's he gone?"

"To git a boat. Says he'll comb thet river till he roots them all out. Let's go git the rest of the boys and head for the river to meet the cap'n."

The two rebels walked south along the road.

Dave hurried back through the woods. Steve had three flat boards in his hands. Scrimshaw was finishing his rough caulking of the boat. He stepped back and shook his head. "Mebbe she'll keep afloat. I don't know for sartain."

"Get a move on," said Dave. "There's a rebel boat coming down the river. I overheard two reb soldiers talking about it, and the boat is skippered by my friend, Cap'n Rance."

"Getting light," said Steve.

They rolled the flimsy skiff over and ran it into the water. They got into it and began to paddle. The sun was showing itself to the east.

"There's the *Southfield!*" said Steve suddenly.

The river mist was slowly dissipating, and they could see the hurricane deck of the sunken craft. There was no one in sight on the deck.

"Listen!" said Scrimshaw.

The soft muffled beating of a steam engine came to them from upriver.

They paddled steadily, and despite the coolness of the dawn air, sweat began to run down their faces. The current forced them close and closer to the *Southfield,* and Dave momentarily expected to hear sharp challenges and the crashing of rifles.

The beating of the engine was louder now, and they

heard a man call out. "We're close to the *Southfield*, Cap'n Rance!"

Scrimshaw steered the leaky skiff close to the wreck and looked back over his shoulder. "In close," he said quietly, "behind the *Southfield*."

They drifted alongside the craft. There was seemingly no one aboard her. The beating of the engine became louder, and they could hear the gurgling of water past the bow of the oncoming boat.

"Tie her up to the *Southfield*!" called out Cap'n Rance.

The picket boat bumped alongside the other side of the wreck, and there was the sound of boots resounding from her decks. "Ain't no one here, Cap'n Rance!" a man called out.

"Them Yankees must have captured the guard," said said Rance.

"Do we stay here, Cap'n Rance?"

"Got to block the river, the cunnel says. They's two or three old schooners being brought down."

The swift current tugged at the skiff. Steve let go his hold, and the skiff drifted swiftly down-river and appeared at the end of the wreck. Scrimshaw stabbed a stubby forefinger toward the low shore, and the two boys paddled with all their strength as they heard the engine of the picket boat cough into life and then settle down to a steady throbbing.

They were fifty feet from the shore when Dave felt water creeping up about his legs. The skiff surged in the flow of the river, and water poured over the sides.

"Abandon ship, all hands," said Scrimshaw.

They rolled over the low sides into the cold water and struck out for the shore. Dave's feet sank into the thick

141

mud as the picket boat appeared beyond the *Southfield*.

"Yankees!" roared a man in the picket boat.

The three fugitives splashed ashore just as a rifle spat flame and smoke. The slug struck a cypress a foot away from Dave.

"Head in! Head in!" yelled Rance hoarsely. "Them's the two Yankees I want! They's a price on their heads!"

The three fugitives plunged into the wet clinging brush and ran like frightened deer through the swamp, splashing through water and mud, careening from trees and fighting breathlessly through the brush.

Rifles popped behind them, and now and then a slug whined its song of death through the air.

Dave knew what was ahead of them: tidal streams, thick and sluggish; cypress trees intertwined with thorny brush; no pathways.

Scrimshaw coughed. He gripped his side. "Go on, mates!" he said thickly.

The two boys grabbed the old sailor by the arms and forced him through the brush as men yelled to each other behind them. They splashed through a shallow muddy stream and dashed into thicker brush. The briars cut like little knives, and their clothing tore into tatters, revealing their bleeding flesh. Dave felt his strength waning. He staggered against a tree and fell heavily. Scrimshaw went down, face foremost, into the stinking mud. Steve leaned against a tree. "I've shot my wad," he said weakly.

Scrimshaw raised his muddy face. "Slip your cables, mates," he said.

The two boys looked at each other. They knew what would happen to them if they were caught, while all that would happen to Scrimshaw would be a term in a rebel prison until the end of the war. But Dave knew Scrimshaw. Prison life would soon kill him, used as he was to the open life of the sea.

" I'm staying, Davie," said Steve.

Dave nodded. He picked up a soggy branch for a weapon and looked back toward the river.

They had stopped firing, but the noise of their progress through the swamp could be heard plainly.

A deer suddenly bounded into the area where the three fugitives were. He reared up on his hind legs and then darted forward right past them, bounding cleanly across the little stream to disappear into the brush, but the noise of his passage could be heard plainly.

" There they go to the southwest, Cap'n Rance! " a soldier yelled.

The noise of the pursuit died away to the southwest.

Dave looked at Steve. " I'll never hunt a deer again as long as I live," he said.

" Amen to that, mate! "

They pulled Scrimshaw to his feet and plodded through the clinging muck toward the northeast.

Chapter 14

THE SUN was up, and the swamp was receiving some of its heat through the thickly intertwining branches of the cypress trees. Now and then a bird twittered from the trees only to fade into silence as the noise of splashing footsteps came through the swamp.

Steve Raintree stopped walking and wiped the sweat from his dirty face. "Where are we, Davie? You got any bearings?"

Dave leaned against a tree. Scrimshaw was making heavy weather through the muck fifty feet behind them. "Close to the Roanoke, I'd say."

"Beats me how you can tell."

Scrimshaw stopped and leaned on his tree-branch staff. He was in bad shape. "I'll need a careening and an overhauling in dry dock," he said.

"I can smell the sound," said Dave.

Steve wrinkled his nose at the fetid smell of the swamp. "Over this? You got a nose like a bloodhound, Davie."

"Don't mention bloodhounds," said Dave.

"Shove off," said Scrimshaw. "I ain't in the mood to stay here. Once I get a heaving deck under my feet I'll feel like a man again."

They went on through the woods until suddenly they

saw the sunlight glinting from open water. They plodded on until they stood on the shore of Batchelor's Bay.

" There's a tug out there! " said Steve.

The little vessel was moving slowly along the shore, trailing a cloud of smoke.

" 'Tis the picket tug *Valley City*! " said Scrimshaw.

Steve stripped off his filthy shirt and attached it to Scrimshaw's staff. He stepped up onto a log and began to wave it back and forth.

" Looks like Stevie is pestered by these flies," said Scrimshaw dryly.

" She's slowing down," said Dave.

A plume of steam shot from the escape pipe as the tug lost way. The sun glinted on the glasses of an officer who stood on the foredeck of the tug. He turned and gave a command. Sailors ran to a cutter and lowered her into the water with a splash, tumbling down into her carrying revolvers and cutlasses. They cast loose and drifted away from the tug. The oars were fitted into their rowlocks, poised, and then began to strike the water together, driving the cutter toward the beach, with sun glinting from the wet oars.

The cutter was fifty yards from shore when the command came. " Way enough! " The oars were lifted from the water, allowing the cutter to drift. " Who are you? " called the officer in the stern sheets.

Dave cupped his hands about his mouth. " Midshipman David Scott, Acting Midshipman Steven Raintree, Ablebodied Seaman Josiah Appleby, U.S.S. *Monticello*. We were with Lieutenant Cushing in Picket Boat Number One."

" Cushing? Where is he? "

The three fugitives looked at each other, hardly daring to say what was in their minds. *Cushing had not returned.*

"We don't know, sir," called out Dave.

The officer sat down. "Stand by to give way," he commanded. "Give way together!"

The cutter surged toward the beach. Fifty feet from the shore the officer stood up again. "Way enough! Hold water!" The cutter lost way and drifted into the shallow water. "Back water all! Way enough! Oars."

The three fugitives splashed out into the water and clambered aboard. "Thank God," said Scrimshaw. He kissed a gunwale. "I'll never go ashore again as long as I live."

"Stand by to give way!" came the command. "Give way together! Hold water port! Pull hard starboard! Give way together!"

The officer looked down at his three passengers. "I'm Acting Master Brooks. We've been looking for men from the expedition. You say you don't know where Cushing is?"

"No," said Dave.

Brooks shook his head. "How did you make out?"

"We reached the ram and exploded the torpedo under her."

"And came out alive?"

"We're here," said Steve.

"Did you sink her?"

Dave shrugged. "She was listing a little the last I saw of her."

"And Cushing?"

Dave looked away. "The last I saw of him he was swimming away from the launch."

They did not speak again until they were in the neat little galley of the tug, drinking steaming coffee and eating beans and soft bread. Scrimshaw emptied his cup and refilled it. "No more gallant seaman ever lived than Will Cushing," he said. He raised his cup. "Here's to him!"

~

Dave stood by the starboard rail of the *Valley City*, looking out across the calm water, thinking of Will Cushing. Steve and Scrimshaw were asleep below. The night was quiet, with only a slight swell on the dark waters. Stars glinted in the sky, but there was no moon. The *Valley City* swung at her anchor in Batchelor's Bay, not far from the wide mouth of the Roanoke River. Dave had tried to sleep, but he had kept thinking of Will Cushing and finally had dressed and come up on deck.

Brooks had sent a message to the *Shamrock*, telling Commander Macomb that he had picked up three survivors of Picket Boat Number One, but that Cushing was unaccounted for.

A seaman came up beside Dave and grounded his Sharps carbine. "Still waiting?" he asked.

"Yes."

"He's too brave to die."

"He's still alive."

The man shrugged. "From what you told us it doesn't seem possible that anyone could have come through that hail of bullets they fired at you."

"*He's still alive!*"

The man raised his head. "I hope so. Listen!"

There was a splashing noise off the starboard quarter. The seaman ran aft, cocking his carbine as he ran. Dave followed him.

147

"Ship ahoy!" the faint hail came across the dark waters.

The seaman turned. "Get Mister Brooks," he said.

"That may be one of our men."

"Aye, and it may *not* be one of our men. The rebels might be trying to blow us up."

Dave aroused Brooks. The crew tumbled out on deck, armed with revolvers, cutlasses, and grenades. A gun was primed and run out.

"Ship ahoy!" the hail came again.

Brooks turned. "Slip the cable! Get under way! Have a boat manned and ready to lower! We can take no chances."

The anchor cable was slipped. The tug had steam up, and she soon got under way in the darkness, with the crew peering out toward the place where they had heard the hail. Scrimshaw and Steve came up on deck.

"Ship ahoy!" The hail sounded desperate this time.

"Who goes there?" challenged Brooks.

"Lieutenant Will Cushing!"

Dave's heart leaped.

"He's dead," called out Brooks. "Stay your distance!"

Dave leaned over the rail. "Bodgo!" he hailed.

"Molly Waldo!"

Dave turned to Brooks. "It's him! It's him, I tell you!"

They could see a small, flat-bottomed, square-ended skiff bobbing in the slight swell. Dave peered closely and saw the long brown hair of the man hanging down over his face. "Mister Cushing!" he yelled.

The *Valley City* came alongside the skiff. Dave, with a heaving line in his hand, jumped down into the skiff and made it fast. He helped lift the exhausted officer over the low rail of the tug and helped carry him into Brooks's cabin. Cushing dropped to the bunk and grinned at Dave. "I knew I'd make it," he said weakly.

He was a mess, covered with mud and scratched and torn by briars. His left hand was bound in a filthy rag. Brooks handed him a steaming cup of coffee. "You're lucky you made it, sir," he said. "Too bad you didn't sink the ram, though."

Cushing grinned again. "No? She's sitting on the bottom in eight feet of water, with a hole in her belly big enough to steam through with this tug, sir! "

Dave yelled. Men at the door had heard what was said, and they began to yell too. A rocket hissed upward to burst in a shower of light. It was followed by another and another, and in the distance could be seen the rest of the squadron.

"Ahoy the *Valley City*! " hailed a seaman aboard the *Commodore Hull.* "What's up? "

"The *Albemarle* has been sunk by Cushing! "

Rockets hissed up from the *Commodore Hull,* and the message was passed from vessel to vessel until the sound was lighted by dozens of soaring rockets that burst with faint popping sounds.

"How did you escape, sir? " asked Scrimshaw of Cushing.

"I struck out downstream once I left the launch. I tried to save Woodward, but the poor fellow went down like a stone. I'm sure Higgins drowned too.

"I managed to reach shore on the Plymouth side of the river and lay there exhausted. When I woke it was daylight, and I was close enough to Plymouth to see the town swarming with soldiers. I heard some soldiers talking but couldn't find out if the ram had been sunk. I made my way through a cypress swamp. You have no idea how hard it is to get through that mud and those briars."

"No, sir," said Steve with a straight face.

"I could see a working party of soldiers sinking schooners to obstruct the channel. About noon I ran into an old Negro. I warned him that Abe Lincoln would skin him if he gave me away. I gave him twenty dollars in sodden greenbacks from my wallet and some texts of Scripture I had, in order to get him to go into Plymouth to see if the ram had been sunk. He was back within the hour and told me the *Albemarle* was indeed sunk and that the rebels would surely hang me to the nearest cypress if they caught me.

"I almost ran into a picket party, but managed to steal their boat, the one I reached the *Valley City* in. I paddled hour after hour until daylight was gone, and reached the mouth of the Roanoke. I steered by a star until I saw this vessel. You know the rest."

"Get some sleep now, sir," said Brooks.

Cushing sat up. "*Now?* No, sir! Get me and my men here aboard the *Shamrock*! There is still work to be done! "

A cutter took them to the flagship, where Cushing reported in to Commander Macomb while rockets still soared through the dark air and the sound of continuous cheering could be heard from the vessels of the little squadron.

Cushing came out on deck and walked to Dave, Scrimshaw, and Steve. "We get under way in the morning," he said with a smile.

"Where away, sir? " asked Dave.

Cushing jerked a thumb. "Up the Roanoke again to try to force a passage to Plymouth."

Steve shook his head. "Well, at least the ram is sunk, and we can fight back from a real fighting ship instead of from Scrimshaw's Ark."

Cushing nodded. "I'd like to see the *Albemarle* sitting on the muddy bottom of the Roanoke, but I'm not sure I'll be here."

"Why, sir?" asked Dave.

"Commander Macomb thinks I should carry a personal report of my success to Admiral Porter at Hampton Roads. He has already sent a picket boat with the news to Roanoke Island. I hope it doesn't get back until after we have recaptured Plymouth."

A lone rocket arched through the dark sky and traced its fiery course until it burst in a shower of sparks. Then the squadron was mantled with darkness again, but there would be little sleep aboard any of the ships that night. Cushing's success had routed sleep from the squadron, and, too, there was the prospect of battle again within a matter of hours. There would be much to do.

Chapter 15

THE MORNING of the thirty-first of October dawned bright and clear. The squadron lay at anchor at the juncture of the Middle River and Roanoke River. They had left Batchelor's Bay on the morning of the twenty-ninth and steamed up the Roanoke to exchange shots with rebel shore batteries, but they had found that the enemy had sunk schooners near the *Southfield*, effectively blocking that passage to Plymouth.

Dave had insisted that the squadron could traverse the Middle River easily enough, as his father's steamer, the *Alice*, drew more draft than any of them and had steamed that way several times before the war. A reconnaissance had proved Dave right.

On the thirtieth the squadron had gone up Middle River, shelling Plymouth across the intervening neck of land, until it had reached the Roanoke. Now, on the morning of the thirty-first, they were to run down the Roanoke River to attack Plymouth. But brave Will Cushing had left the squadron on the thirtieth aboard the *Valley City* en route to Hampton Roads.

The crews of the vessels were getting ready for the attack. The squat ferryboat, the *Commodore Hull,* was to lead the way, as her construction allowed her to fire dead ahead. The *Whitehead,* which had just arrived with stores and munitions for the squadron, was lashed alongside the *Tacony,* while the tugs *Bazley* and *Belle* were lashed to the *Shamrock* and *Otsego* to provide motive power in case of accident to the engines of the double-enders. The *Wyalusing* was to steam in alone.

Decks had been cleared for action. Guns had been shotted and primed and run out. Boarding nets had been rigged. Cutlasses, revolvers, carbines, and grenades had been issued to the crews. Steam was up in all the vessels. Three bells of the forenoon watch had just been struck aboard the *Shamrock* when the signal flags crept up. " Go ahead fast! " was the command on all the vessels.

Smoke gushed up, the exhausts began to labor, and the water purled back from the bows as the squadron steamed down the Roanoke past Warren's Neck. Almost instantly the guns of Fort Gray opened up on them, but the heavy guns of the Union vessels soon drove the rebels from their posts.

Gun and funnel smoke mingled together and hung over the squadron as they approached Welch's Creek and were taken under fire by the guns of the fort built by the Union forces and captured by the Confederates.

Dave was stationed at one of the broadside nine-inch Dahlgren guns of the *Shamrock,* while Steve was stationed at the gun next to Dave's. Scrimshaw was at the wheel of the double-ender.

A shore battery near Plymouth began to spout smoke and flames, and was answered by the crashing broadsides of the *Shamrock.* Smoke blew back on Dave as the gun was run in, loaded, primed, and run out again to be fired, run in, loaded, primed, and run out again, with the precision of a drill team. The double-ender shuddered now and then as shot struck her. Spouts of water spurted up from the river and deluged the gunners, but it didn't faze them a bit as they fought stripped to the waist, dripping with sweat and river water and blackened by powder smoke.

Minié bullets thudded into the superstructure of the *Shamrock* as rebel sharpshooters fired at the laboring gun crews.

Now all the Confederate batteries were roaring in defiance to the crashing broadsides of the vessels. Sharpshooters fired from houses and from behind trees, and here and there a seaman dropped to the deck. Shell, grape, and canister tore and whistled through the smoky air like the rushing of vast coveys of grouse or partridge.

Dave stepped back as the gun roared back into recoil. Something down-river caught his eyes. It was the *Albemarle,* resting on the bottom, with her carapace showing above the water. Not a gun was fired from her. Dave looked back at Steve and grinned. " There she is! " he yelled.

" Look alive there, reefer! " yelled Dave's gun commander. Dave jumped aside as the Dahlgren spat flame and smoke and reared back. The shell struck full into the center of the rebel fort and was followed by a tremendous explosion that hurled dirt and timbers high into the air atop a gush of flame and gas.

" The magazine! The magazine! " roared the gun captain.

Smoke hung low over the battery as the debris settled

about it. The rebel guns had stopped firing. Then suddenly the sweating crewmen could see the rebel gunners abandoning the battery and running into the woods behind Plymouth.

There was a little more sporadic firing from the town, and then it died away as shells smashed into the houses.

"Cease firing!" came the command.

The guns were shotted and primed and run out. The echoes died away in the woods, and the smoke drifted off on the wind. The sudden silence almost seemed to hurt Dave's ears.

The squadron steamed slow ahead until they were opposite the smoke-shrouded town. Anchors plunged into the water, and the vessels turned slowly until they were facing upstream.

"Boats away!" came the command.

The landing parties were ready. Boats dropped to the water to the sound of whirring falls and whining blocks, and the landing parties tumbled into them, armed to the teeth. Swiftly the boats converged toward the sagging wharves and came alongside; they were made fast, and the crews clambered out onto the wharves and formed into parties. Then they moved slowly toward the center of the town, flushing rebel stragglers.

Dave stopped on the main street and looked up and down. Smoke drifted from a burning house. A scrawny dog scuttled off with its tail between its legs. The Stars and Stripes was run up into the breeze, and a steady cheering began from the seamen ashore and from those on the vessels.

Dave picked up a trampled Confederate flag and folded it, placing it inside his coat. He heard a man talking rapidly to an officer. Dave whirled. It was Cap'n Rance, but his filthy shell jacket was gone and so was his bedraggled slouch hat with its disreputable feather. He wore a dented plug hat and a cutaway coat. "Yes, sirree," he was saying. "Couldn't wait until you-uns got back here to old Plymouth. I'm a pro-Union man, suh. Glad to hev yuh back."

Steve Raintree stood behind a post watching Rance, and he was grinning with delight as he saw Dave. He jerked a thumb toward Rance. "Real Yankee-lover, ain't he?"

Dave moved closer.

Rance waved his arms. "Them rebels give us Union men a hard time, suh, a hard, hard time. Now I kin help yuh any way yuh like. Know the country like a book. Kin help yuh flush out these secesh people as soon as yuh want me to. 'Course I don't expect nothin', but if you was to see that I was compensated, so to speak, I'd be mortal obliged."

Dave took out the flag. "Cap'n Rance!" he called out. "Did you drop this flag?"

Rance whirled. His face dropped. "What do you mean, suh?"

"Why, Cap'n Rance! Don't you know me?"

Rance sprinted toward an alleyway. Steve whistled softly as he threw his carbine in between Rance's churning legs. The man hit the ground hard and Steve sat down on him. "Your prisoner, Davie," he said. "Too bad for the Confederacy. Old Marse Robert E. Lee is sure going to miss his right-hand man . . . Cap'n Rance."

~

The supply steamer *Rhode Island* plunged and wallowed through rough cross seas off Cape Fear, trailing a

156

raveled scarf of smoke. A cold November wind held the sails as hard as marble. Far to the south could be seen the topsails of another vessel which was approaching the *Rhode Island* on a converging course.

Midshipmen Dave Scott and Steve Raintree stood at the weather rail, watching the other vessel. Steve had been appointed a full-fledged midshipman for his part in the destruction of the *Albemarle*.

Boatswain Scrimshaw Appleby swayed down the pitching deck, muffled in his thick peacoat. He stopped beside the two reefers. " Can ye make her out? " he asked.

" No," said Dave.

They stood there in the keening wind, watching the other vessel. " 'Tis the *Monticello*! " said Scrimshaw. " I'd know her by the cut of her sails, for I've mended them many a time with palm and needle."

Dave grinned. The three of them had received orders at Roanoke Island to report back to their own ship, the swift *Monticello*.

" Blockading duty again," grumbled Scrimshaw. " Wet berths, moldy sea biscuit, and hard salt horse. Who wouldn't sell a farm and go to sea? "

Steve winked at Dave. " Maybe you're getting too old, Scrimshaw, to stay at sea with us young fellers."

" Hah, I'll hand, reef, and steer long after ye two reefers are retired as admirals! "

The *Monticello* drew closer. Cushing was in Washington, waiting for orders, but he had sent a letter to the three of them with good news. He had been promoted to lieutenant commander to date as of October 27, 1864, the date of the destruction of the *Albemarle,* and was now the youngest lieutenant commander in the Navy. Prize money of about eighty thousand dollars, which was to be apportioned out to the officers and men who had been with Cushing, had been awarded for the *Albemarle*. But the best news was that Gideon Welles, Secretary of the Navy, had appointed both Dave and Steve to the United States Naval Academy, which they were to enter at the termination of hostilities in order to further their careers in the Navy. Scrimshaw had been promoted to boatswain. All of them were to serve aboard the *Monticello*.

There was still much work for the North Atlantic Blockading Squadron. Fort Fisher, which kept Wilmington open for the blockade-runners, was to be reduced and captured, and the *Monticello* was sure to participate in the action both by sea with its heavy guns, and by land with sailors acting as infantry. The war was not yet over.

The *Monticello* rounded into the wind, and sailors swarmed aloft to heave her to. It was done with precision. The captain of the *Rhode Island* spoke from his quarterdeck. " Smartly done," he said in admiration.

Steve shrugged. "We'll see to it that it's done a little more smartly once we report aboard for duty, eh, mates? "

" Bodgo! " said Scrimshaw.

" Molly Waldo! " said Dave.

Sources for This Book

DAVID SCOTT, his father Micah, Steven Raintree, Captain Rance, and Scrimshaw Appleby are fictitious characters in this story. The blockade-runner *Phantom* is also fictitious. It was not unusual in Civil War times for a boy to do a man's job; nor were older men and partially disabled men like Micah Scott prevented from fighting.

Much of the research material of ROANOKE RAIDERS comes from *Battles and Leaders of the Civil War* (Century, 1887), of which I have the volumes reprinted by Thomas Yoseloff, Inc., in 1957. Volume IV of *Battles and Leaders* furnished material on the construction of the ram *Albemarle* and her armament; the fight between the *Albemarle* and the *Sassacus;* and the destruction of the *Albemarle* by Commander Cushing from his own account.

The United States Navy (From the Revolution to Date) (P. F. Collier & Son, 1917), furnished photographs and drawings of vessels mentioned in the book. *A Sailor's Treasury*, by Frank Shay and Edward A. Wilson (W. W. Norton & Company, Inc., 1951), furnished sailor lore and lingo of great value to the author. Detailed information on the blockade-runners was taken from *Blockade*, by Robert

Carse (Rinehart & Company, Inc., 1958).

Other sources were the *Official Records of the Union* and *Confederate Navies in the War of the Rebellion;* the Los Angeles Public Library; the Chicago Public Library; the Newberry Library of Chicago. Many other books too numerous to mention, have gone into the making of ROANOKE RAIDERS.

William Barker Cushing died a young man, at the age of thirty-two, but he was known throughout the United States Navy as " Albemarle " Cushing. As is customary to-day in the United States Navy, a destroyer was named after him. In World War Two, at the naval Battle of Guadalcanal during the night action of November 12-13, 1942, the leading destroyer and the first into action was the U.S.S. *Cushing.* She did not survive the battle.

The author first read about Will Cushing about thirty-five years ago as a boy in Chicago whose one dream was to graduate from Annapolis. That dream never came true, but the story of Will Cushing remained with him until this book was written.